HOME IS WHERE THE HURT IS

A PSYCHOLOGICAL THRILLER NOVEL

K. G. JESSUP

WARNING

This book contains depictions of domestic violence. Reader discretion is advised.

To all the lives lost,
to those still living through it,
to those finding the courage to leave,
and to those rebuilding a life free from fear—
this book is for you.
You are seen, believed, and not alone.
Even in ruin, you will bloom again.

1

____

THROUGH THE WINDOW
MIRANDA

Her life used to be mine. And I loved it, while it lasted.

But nothing lasts forever.

The brevity of Hunter Brannigan's love is only matched by his temper. In the end, it's what tore our marriage and family apart. The roaring flames of the fire pit consumed every reminder of me. Photographs, books, letters, even extravagant dresses, discarding me from both his memory and my baby's. Only flecks of ash remain now, after all these years. It's a far cry from when we sat there sipping merlot along with his executive friends and their wives, debating which country to holiday in this year.

It didn't surprise me, though. He treats others with far less care, both professionally and personally.

Even his own parents couldn't escape it. He abandoned them in the wake of his mother's dementia diagnosis. And his best friend and business partner of his very first venture. They went all in, but Hunter's betrayal left him high and dry while Hunter's new company raked in seven figures per year in its first five years. It's baffling how he can walk away so easily. And then there's me. Will he discard this one, too?

Sometimes I like to watch her. This new one. This replacement.

She didn't know. At least I didn't think she does.

From the other side of the window, hidden beneath the shadows of a Jacaranda tree; I watch Marlys race down the stairwell, running her polished fingernails along the white banister, skipping every second step. She brushes past the home office where Hunter, glued to his phone, paces across the room. Her perfect, broad smile makes me sick to my stomach. So innocent, so unaware.

Marlys drapes the floral print apron from her neck and sets about making batter, before flopping pancakes into a neat stack.

"Kage, breakfast is ready," she calls out.

Dusting her hands against the fabric, she grabs a mug announcing, Number one dad. I'd bet my last dollar, if I had any, that she bought that. Steam rises from it as she heads towards the office door. She knocks, awaiting Hunter's approval to enter. He nods. Smiling still, she pats his shoulder while his focus remains fixed on his call.

Again, she calls out to my son just as the doorbell rings. The family's black cat, Liquorice, is curled in the warmth of their handsome neighbour's arms, bundling her like a baby.

I strain to hear their muted conversation, but the glass barrier and distance between us muffles their voices, barely able to hear their laughter. But there's no doubt Marlys' god-awful grin is even broader than before. He mirrors her, inching closer as her hand grazes against his arm. This is a side of Xander I haven't seen before. He never flirted with me like this, that's for sure. And in all honesty, I thought he was gay. Not that I'm in any position to judge.

It's a curious thing to think you know a person. But even if you knew someone for a century, I think they would still hold something back, whether through shame, or guilt, or some other wretched feeling. You can't truly know anyone else. Not really.

My chest tightens as Kage ambles towards the table. He was so young when we parted. Barely able to take a step. Now he's almost a giant, at six feet tall, and always glued to his phone, just like his father. And so broody. I suppose that's teenagers, though.

He slides into a chair at the breakfast table, facing the window where I'm precariously positioned. Marlys places a neat pile of pancakes before him and smiles. How does her face not fall off from all that excessive grinning? It's beyond me. Kage disregards her and drowns the plate in a sea of maple.

But then her smile falters. Just for a moment. She discreetly wipes away a tear from beneath her eye as she turns back towards the kitchen. She closes her eyes briefly and then opens them, putting that smile back on her face.

And there it is. The hint that tells me what I'm itching to know.

She's not Cinderella, and this isn't her castle.

Nevertheless, I'm familiar with her routine, and I observe her while she makes lunch for both Hunter and Kage. Grabbing the stack of brightly coloured post-it notes, she scribbles something before placing them on the meals she's so lovingly prepared. She's so pleased with herself. It should be me placing the note, not her. If only I could, I would tell Kage how much I love him. That my heart bursts with just the memory of us. But a mother shouldn't have to yearn. To be so close and yet, unable to touch him, torture.

The little black cat, so elegant, crawls along the table's

edge, pouncing onto the window ledge. I can't have her bringing any attention to me. I slither further back into the mottled shadows of overhanging branches, behind a row of thick Gardenia brush. She balances, stretching her hind leg like a ballerina, and bathes in the sliver of sunshine penetrating through the glass. When she's done, she curves her spine with a yawn, and steps forward, but then she sees me, and her eyes lock with mine.

She jerks into a defensive position, mouth pulling back into a high-pitched hiss. Kage glances over at the interruption, furrowing his brow, but he's none the wiser and quickly returns his attention to his phone and pancakes.

Holding the cat's stare, I crouch deeper into the shadows, as far as I can to hide. Yet she takes a daring step forward, challenging me as her hissing grows louder and more aggressive.

This blasted cat will give me away one of these days.

A gust of wind bursts through the garden, branches and bushes rustling. My opportunity to flee. I scramble from the window to another spot to wait, closer to the garage, burrowed into a hedge of Murraya's. While I rest, memories recoil, too painful to endure. But I need to monitor Kage and his parents—if you can call them that.

The front door swings open as Marlys heads towards the small Toyota hybrid, a birthday present from Hunter. Kage follows behind, swinging his bag over his shoulder, and dragging himself towards the front passenger door. He stands, waiting for the beep. If I reach out now, I can touch him, feel my son's warmth. But do I dare? What if I frighten him? I can't.

Withdrawing from the bush's edge, he reaches for the door handle, but he shudders, as if an icy chill ran down his back. His eyes narrow as he turns, scanning the vicinity for a moment, then shakes his head to clear it before jumping in the car.

That was close. Too close.

I'll have to be more careful next time.

2

INSIDE

MIRANDA

I crawl into the dead space beneath the stairwell, ensuring I leave no trace of my presence. Then I wait.

At the back, nestled in a tight nook between stacked boxes, I find an ideal spot. The family rarely comes in here, so I know I'm safe for now.

My head throbs, the pain growing stronger and pulsing louder with each passing moment. I've been here before, but never felt this way. A wave of nausea flows through me.

I squint into the inky blackness, broken only by slivers of light at the door's edge. There's nothing here that could cause this. Being careful not to move anything, I peek around the boxes, with neatly folded flaps secured by clear packing tape. Hidden away is a partially opened box. I don't remember seeing that before.

An urge compels me. My will wars against my curiosity.

Don't touch it. Don't leave any evidence. But the urge overpowers my caution.

I try to reach it, but it's impossible. As I inch closer, a sharp, stinging sensation surges through me, jolting me to my core. It's a mix of electricity and déjà vu. Whatever's inside is mine. I know it.

Footsteps climb the staircase above me, pulling me back. *Stay quiet. Don't move.* I remain rooted in place until the last member of the household leaves. After counting to ten, I creak open the door to my hiding place and crawl out into the sprawling, eerily quiet lounge room.

It's awkwardly familiar, despite the change of wall colour since I lived here, and the updated couch. The memories burn as they flash through my mind. Both happy and hateful, all simultaneously.

On tiptoe, I approach the long side table filled with different sized frames. Each one holds a different memory of Marlys' shared life with Hunter and Kage. Our photographs once took centre stage, yet the only thing that links me to it now is the colour of my son's eyes. Blue as the ocean. He got that from me.

A trail follows my fingertip along the edge, through the light film of dust. I can't help the hollow laugh that spills from me. Marlys clearly lacks the discipline to maintain a house to his standards. It's surprising that she hasn't experienced his ire with such careless work. Perhaps I missed it, or else she can expect it soon.

I'm drawn to the window again. Standing, staring across the garden, towards Xanders house. But I'm pulled from my thoughts by Liquorice's hiss. Her hair is raised along her thin spine.

Escaping the feline, I move to Hunter's office. Through the glass squares of the French doors, she monitors me, but I ignore her. She can't hurt me now.

Messy piles of papers fill the large desk, spilling onto the floor where he's orchestrated smaller piles, likely for work. A business takeover, perhaps? But this isn't what I wanted to explore.

I head up the stairs, slowly and elegantly, running my fingertips along that same white banister Marlys did earlier. The irony pits in my stomach.

To Kage's room, I set off, picking up my pace a little, eager to know him better.

Kage's bedroom has a strange aura about it. Melancholy and anger.

I settle on his bed, burying my face into his pillow. It's the closest I've come to wrapping my arms around him, and I squeeze his pillow as his surrogate. Breathing in his scent, tears well, and I lay on the plush comforter, taking in every piece of him that I can.

From this angle, the ceiling looks like the night sky, midnight blue dotted with long forgotten glow in the dark stars. NBA players and Xbox games fill his walls, and a school semester calendar hangs above his desk, where his laptop sits open. Scattered clothes sit in bunches on the floor, and desk drawers partially open. I don't want to be a snoop, but I want to know him more intimately.

Reaching for the third drawer's handle, the pain from earlier returns. I recoil at the sensation, but it also urges me forward. Does he have something of mine in here? A small souvenir of his mother, perhaps.

Old birthday cards and papers with notes about detention intermingle with knick-knacks from cereal boxes and collector cards. But under all the remnants is a small stack of photographs. *Oh, my word.*

My heart sinks as I rub my thumb over the first picture. A newborn photo of Kage, wrapped in a pale green blanket, with matching cap. I recall the memory, taken in the hospital. He was a mere six hours old, small and fragile. Set in stone as the best day of my life.

Setting it aside, I take in the next one. It's another of Kage, at around three months old. Sitting in my lap, filling my arms. I can almost hear Kage's bubbles of laughter. I'm surprised Hunter let him keep this token. This tiny token of us. I place it with the other and move onto the third and final picture.

Older than the last two, this one is from my high school days. My makeup consists of neutrals and pinkish browns—the popular look during my senior year in the late nineties. And my formal dress is a sleek number, red satin flowing from my chest to my heels, cinched in at the waist. *How did he find this?*

I take in each reflection from the past, splayed out on the desk. But the baby photo of Kage is the one that holds my attention. Raising the memento to my lips, I press a tender kiss to the spot where his chubby little cheeks are, then hold it to my heart as if it were him.

A banging sound reverberates through the house, knocking me from my reverie. Loud thumping escalates as it follows the stairs upwards. Panic sets in. Reeling with anxiety, I need to hide, but where? I glance around, feverishly searching. They're already on the landing.

Shit! The closet.

I dash inside and swiftly pull the door closed just as the bedroom door opens, thudding against the wall before slamming shut. My heart beats furiously, hoping and praying that he doesn't find me.

The photos. I left them on the desk.

I hear Kage raging around his room. But then the pacing seems to become quieter, and his footsteps move toward my hiding place.

The closet door creaks open. I withdraw further into the corner.

I can't let him see me. Not like this.

3

CUTTING IT CLOSE
MIRANDA

Anxiety grips me as the door to the closet creaks ajar. Rapping at the bedroom door draws Kage's attention.

"What?" he says in a gruff tone.

"Can we talk about this please?" a muffled female voice says from the other side of the door.

"Just go away."

I peek through the narrow gap between the closet doors as Kage throws himself on the bed, plasters a pillow against his face, and screams into it.

I want to burst from the closet and comfort him. Bring his head to my shoulder and stroke his hair and ask him what's wrong. Given the time of day, Kage should be at school still. I focus my attention on the conversation, eager to find out what's eating at him. There's nothing I can do, but the worry will only eat at me if it remains undiscovered.

Another gentle rap on the door.

"Kage. Honey," Marlys says. Her voice is no longer muffled, and I suspect she's standing in the doorway now.

He pulls the pillow closer, tighter, growling into it.

Her footsteps are light as air as she approaches the bed. She sits propped on the edge beside Kage.

"Can we talk about what happened, please?"

"It doesn't matter. Just forget about it," he retorts. But she isn't giving up that easily and reaches for the pillow. He grabs it tighter and rolls away from her, onto his side.

With slumped shoulders, Marlys sucks in a breath. "I'm on your side here, Kage. Let me help you."

Kage guffaws, unconvinced. In one swift move, he sits upright, legs bent, and wraps his arms around his knees.

"You're not my mother. And you can't un-suspend me. So, tell me, what is it you think you can do to help me, *Marlys*?" His voice is thick with sarcasm. And while I'll always side with my son, his arrogance gives me pause.

She lowers her voice a little. "If you tell me what happened, I might be able to speak with the principal and get this whole mess sorted out."

"You think I'm worried about being suspended?" Kage retorts. "I couldn't care less about that."

Marlys clears her throat and straightens her posture.

"Would you rather have this conversation with your father?"

Kage's eyes narrow, lips drawing together tightly. She's hit a nerve.

"Fuck you, Marlys." His impropriety appals me. I would never allow such disrespect in my home. But then again, that's what she gets for trying to play mother. He darts off the bed and storms out of the room, leaving her alone. She's not actually alone, is she? No. I'm here too. Watching.

Moments later, the front door slams shut.

Once she gets out of here, I can too. Before I'm caught.

But she doesn't move. Sitting there, she sobs into her hands.

When she stops sobbing, with the back of her hand she wipes her nose, before fingertips clear the tears from her cheeks and eyes.

"What am I even doing here?" Marlys mumbles. "You hate me. And I'll let you in on a little secret —I'm pretty sure your dad is cheating on me." She sighs, then stands. Moving past the desk, she trails a hand over the curve of the chair. Noticing the photos still spread out, she picks one up.

"Look at you, so small. Those chubby cheeks. I wish I'd known you then. Maybe if you had, then you wouldn't hate me so much now." Marlys lets out another sigh, shoulders slumping.

"But you don't need me." She shakes her head. "You need your real mother, not some miserable fill-in like me." Another sob emits from her. "I mean, who am I kidding, really? I'm not parent material. Lord knows I've tried and failed. No, you deserve so much better."

She pulls the photo closer. "Maybe you'd both be better off without me."

As she puts the photo back on the desk, she turns around slowly, surveying the room, before dragging herself back towards the door. With the click of the handle, she's gone.

I'm not sure what to make of all of that. On the one hand, I despise the woman who's taken my place in the family. But on the other, a spark of empathy. I don't like it one bit. Why should I feel sorry for her? I owe her nothing. Then again, she spoke from the heart, not knowing anyone could hear her. And as for that part, an uneasy feeling settles within me. Despite my ire and dislike of Marlys, I've intruded on her as if I'd read the most personal parts of her journal. The part that holds her innermost secrets. Never intended for another. Perhaps it's pity.

Quietly, I sneak out of the wardrobe and slip from Kage's bedroom. I carefully navigate the hallway towards the master bedroom, where I hear crying. The door is slightly ajar, and I peek through. She must be in the ensuite since she's not in plain sight. Her sobs grow fainter as the sound of water splashing against tile begins. A long, hot soak in that very bathtub always helped drown my sorrows, too. But enough of that.

She's distracted now. It's my opportunity to see what Hunter has been hiding. Bedside tables flank their king-sized bed, almost identical except for a small vase of silk roses on one. That must be hers. I go to the other side and open the top drawer. This is unquestionably Hunter's. It's filled with coins, business cards likely discarded from his wallet, a pair of cufflinks, and a motivational business book. Not surprising, given his love of podcasts by that same author. I always thought those were more arrogance than inspiration. Closing the drawer, I open the one below it. Filled with bric-à-brac, there's nothing of interest for me here. Perhaps his underwear drawer?

"Hello?" Marlys calls out from the bathroom. The shower stops. "Hunter, is that you?"

I drop to the floor between the far side of the bed and the far wall. Their bed is an ensemble, so there's no hiding beneath it. But I can still see through the two-inch gap between the floor and bottom of the bed.

A splash comes from the bathroom, then her toes appear at the edge of the tile, where the carpet meets.

"That's odd," she mutters, then moves to the door, inching it open. "Hunter? Kage?" she cries down the hallway. She's met with only her voice vibrating back at her.

Footsteps, then another splash tells me she's soaking again.

This spot won't keep me safe.

If I want to avoid being caught, I need to move—now. I dart behind the thick drapes. Like a statue, I remain until she's finished and dressed.

Now go downstairs, please, Marlys.

Instead, she throws herself on the bed and closes her eyes.

This is ridiculous! What woman her age takes afternoon naps?

Nevertheless, I have no choice but to put up with it. The room is silent and still. Not even humming from the air-conditioner or whirring of the ceiling fan can be heard.

From the stillness, Marlys whispers harshly. "I know someone's there."

A long few minutes pass before she whispers again. Quieter than before, she says, "Who are you?"

She has no clue. And even if she does, there's no way I'm answering and giving myself away. I'm not a complete fool.

Marlys clears her throat. "Amelia? Is it you?"

4

____

IN THE STILLNESS
MARLYS

My skin is still slick from the bath. Even the finest of hairs stand to attention, and my toes curl just like they did as a child, fretting over monsters under the bed. A heavy stillness presses down on me as I lay on the bed. I'm sure I heard someone in here before rummaging around. Yet now the quiet is almost eerie. Listening hard, I close my eyes and focus. Nothing. Just the breeze through the cracks of the windowpane. I suck in a deep breath, holding it before releasing it.

I'm a fraud. Or at least it feels that way. More often than not these days. The evil stepmother, stealing someone else's story—someone else's life. Married to another woman's husband.

None of it is true. My head knows it even if my heart paints a different picture. Yet I don't feel any better for it.

A faint breeze slips through the cracked window, teasing the edges of the curtains. They ripple inward, a slow, deliberate movement that catches my eye. For a moment, I freeze, my breath lodged in my throat. Then a sharper gust whistles through, carrying with it a cold that crawls over my skin like unseen fingers. My heart picks up pace, beating faster as if I'd consumed ten cups of coffee. I don't know what it is but my instincts say to run. To get out of here. Now.

I leap from the bed, bare feet landing on the plush carpet. Hurriedly, I pull on the clothes I laid out earlier, hands trembling with an urgency I can't explain. Three quick strides towards the bedroom door, yanking it open so hard the handle strikes the plaster with a thud. I flinch, heart hammering still, almost expecting something or someone to step into view.

Without another thought, I run on tiptoe, muted footsteps along the hall until I reach the top step, almost overbalancing. Reaching out, I grip the rail, jarring backwards. The pounding in my chest amplifies like a drum. I sense something behind me, shivering my shoulders as I sneak a look. The hallway remains empty. I race down the stairs to the lounge room, switching the television on to distract myself from the quiet, the loneliness, and all the questions that race through my mind.

There are some rooms that I don't enter anymore simply because it doesn't feel right. The energy is off, but I can't put my finger on it. It's the same way I felt upstairs, but I've never felt it in there before. Maybe I'm reading too much into it, or maybe I'm just losing my damn mind.

I collapse onto the couch, legs folding beneath me like they've forgotten how to stand. The television does little to drown out the oppressive quiet of this house—or rather, this mausoleum. The silence here isn't peaceful; it's waiting. It lingers in the corners, stretches along the hallways, presses against the walls until the smallest creak or whisper feels like a scream.

At night, it's even more unsettling.

I knew Hunter was dedicated to his job, but I didn't realise how little time he'd have for Kage and me. Most days, I'm lost amongst the cavernous rooms that fill this place. Even the family I'd willingly adopted feels like a job now. I'm nothing but a full-time nanny to a hormonal teen who detests me, a housekeeper expected to dust even the slightest speck, and an afterthought, summoned only when desire outweighs distraction.

The hairs on my arms lift as I glance at the window. The curtains flutter in the faint breeze, but there's something off about the way they move—too slow, too deliberate. My reflection stares back at me from the glass, pale and wide-eyed, but just as I turn away, I swear I see a shadow pass behind me in the dim light. I whirl around, my heart pounding, but the room is empty, silent except for the whisper of the wind.

Heading to the kitchen, I pick up my phone, unplugging it from its charger before flipping to my messages. I tap out a text and hit send.

ME

Are you free?

A few seconds later, another pops up on the screen.

XANDER

Sure am.

I don't bother replying. Grabbing the house keys from the ceramic bowl on the counter, I shoving them in my pocket, then slip on some ballet flats. As I approach the front door, the feeling returns. A Cold, prickling sensation. It wraps around my neck and pulls tight. My pulse quickens. The room feels smaller somehow, shadows deeper.

I throw the door open with startling force, slamming it shut behind me.

Five minutes later, I'm sitting at one end of his large couch, turned to face him, while he faces me from the other end. One of Xander's arms rests along the back of the couch, while he holds coffee in the other.

"Why don't you just leave him if you're not happy, Marlys?" Xander says. He leans back into the plush blue couch, fingers tightening ever so slightly around his coffee cup.

"You know why," I say, my voice quieter than I meant it to be. The defeat in it makes me wince, but I don't look away from him.

"Kage is a big boy. He'll survive."

I shake my head. "In boarding school, perhaps. But what life is that?"

Xander raises his brow. "It didn't hurt me one bit. Besides, it builds resilience."

Raising my mug with both hands, I take in a long sip, contemplating the suggestion. It's a nice idea, starting over, living my life on my own terms again. But what had that brought me before? Struggling paycheque to paycheque, working a dead-end job as a temp, moving from job to job every other week or month when I scored a decent contract. No, at least with Hunter I have security and a beautiful house to live in, even if I'm lonely most of the time. But that's what I have Xander for. To vent, to listen, to provide me comfort and to help me make sense of this life I never knew before I met the Brannigans.

"He's already been through so much, though."

He furrows a brow. "None of that is your doing."

I sigh. "I know. It's just he deserves better than what he's been given."

"I don't understand why you're rooting for a kid that doesn't show you one ounce of respect, Marlys. You deserve better than that."

Nodding, he's right, of course. "We just haven't bonded yet. That's all. I'm sure he'll come around, eventually. It's just going to take some time."

"How long are you willing to wait? It's already been a year. I would've given up six months ago, if it were me."

"I don't know, Xander. My gut keeps telling me to hold on a little longer. He's been through so much, and he's clearly got trust issues with his mother abandoning him like she did. I can't even imagine how much that would screw with a child's mind."

His brows rise as he deliberates on my argument. "Maybe you're right, Marlys."

Xander sets his coffee down with a soft clink, leaning forward slightly. "But you deserve better." His gaze locks onto mine, voice low, almost coaxing. "You shouldn't have to live like this—alone, waiting for someone to notice you. I notice you." The weight of his words lingers. My stomach twists—not entirely unpleasant but unsettling all the same.

"So," I say, forcing a lighter tone as I sit up straighter. "I haven't seen you 'round much lately. New girlfriend?"

Xander shifts uncomfortably in his seat, furrowing his brows. "Girlfriend?" he says, tipping his head curiously. "Definitely not." He runs a hand through his greying hair like he's trying to figure out what to say. "Just work stuff."

"Oh, I didn't realise you were back at work?" I ask, taking another sip. "I thought you were in early retirement?"

"I am, or was, rather." He shakes his head. "It's just a bit of casual work. Helps keep my mind busy."

"Right." Given he lives alone, I can imagine my brief presence every now and again isn't much to keep him busy.

"I should get back." I glance at my watch.

He nods, following me to the door. Opening it, I step out onto the stoop, as he leans against the frame. "Well, I'm here for you. Be safe."

"Thanks, Xander," I say, flashing a sheepish grin before heading back to the footpath. I give another wave, then stroll towards my house.

My shoes slap against the concrete footpath. When I reach the mailbox, something urges me to look up at the first floor. It's weird, and without reason. Shaking my head, I scold myself. I'm letting my mind run away from me again. But even so, the darkened windows exude a weariness that makes my pulse rise. Then I see it. A tall, slender shape moves behind the sheer curtains in the centre of the frame. Squinting, I dare it to appear again. The sound of a car throttling three doors down interrupts my focus, disturbing the street's ' usual quietude.

Black as night, matching tint on the windows, a newer model SUV crawls down the street. It pauses outside of my house. It's unfamiliar, and occupants hide in plain sight. I don't recognise it, but I wave, trying to break the tension, waiting for the window to roll down. But it doesn't. The car's engine revs, and tires squeal before rushing off, back down the street.

Who was that? What do they want?

Fumbling with the keys, I hurry inside, locking the deadbolt before resting my back against the door.

"Kage?" I call out, but even I can hear the quiver in my voice, strained. But there's no reply. There never is.

The silence is the house is even heavier in the growing evening. Thick and wrong. Reaching for the light switch, I pray it will ease the unnerving sensation, but it doesn't help. For a long moment, I stand in the entryway, breath shallow, every nerve on edge, waiting. For a sound. Or a shadow. Some sort of reaction. Anything.

But nothing comes. Just the oppressive quiet, pressing in on me. Squeezing me. Suffocating me.

Yet the silence feels alive—watching, waiting, just out of sight.

Then, in the stillness, I hear it, the faintest sound. A breath that isn't mine.

5

____

BEHIND CLOSED DOORS

MARLYS

I t's almost midnight, and I haven't heard a word from Kage. My skin crawls, wondering what he's up to out there. He usually goes to his friend's place when things get a little heated, like earlier today, but he should've been home hours ago. If I call, he won't answer. Maybe I'll send a text. Just to see if he's alright. But will he even bother getting back to me? It seems unlikely at best.

Staring at my phone, still resting in my hand, stomach twisting in knots, a rattling piques my attention. It settles, then starts again. More fervent than before. My thoughts rush back to the SUV. Adrenaline takes hold, freezing me in place.

I turn towards the door, heart pounding in my chest. The door rattles as if fists bang against it, over and over again, demanding to be let in. The door reverberates on its hinges.

I can't recall doing anything to warrant this. And nothing Kage could have done at school, would either. But I wouldn't put it past Hunter. When it comes to him and his business, nothing and no one is off limits.

What am I supposed to do? I can barely protect myself, let alone my step-son. And what if they have weapons? It wouldn't take much effort to break this door down, even with all the locks. And then what? A single bullet, a grab of my wrist, and I'd be done for. Hunter should be here. To protect his wife and child. But could he even navigate a volatile danger like that? Maybe if they were vulnerable women, but against a strong male? His daggers are his words; manipulation, the bullets shooting, taking down his opponents. In business, he stands a good chance, but one on one, I doubt it. The only thing keeping them from me and Kage is this one-inch-thick piece of wood and a few pieces of brass tacked onto it.

My phone vibrates in my hand, startling me. I forgot I was even holding it. The message is from Kage, as unlikely as that seems. "Open the door."

Relief unveils me, but my hands still shake. Of course, the deadbolt. Even with a key, Kage couldn't get in. Knowing it's just him, I should feel relieved, but the tension remains as I rush to the door, fumbling with the locking mechanism.

"Just a sec," I say, hoping to soothe his ire before things escalate further.

A heavy groan sneaks through the crack and I'm almost certain he growls, "Hurry up."

The door swings open, and I flash a cowardly grin.

"Hey," I say with arms wide open.

"What'd you lock the deadbolt for?" he asks, scowling as he brushes past me.

"Security." I don't want to scare him by telling him about the SUV this afternoon. He might be a broody teen, but he's still a child. "Have you eaten?"

"I'm fine," he huffs, then stomps up the stairs.

I sigh, shoulders slumping. At least I tried. I just wish he would let me in. What will it take to get through to him?

Resting a hand on the bottom of the banister, I watch until Kage disappears from sight. The silence is heavier after he leaves, like it's reclaiming the space left behind.

Back in the lounge room, I switch off the television, and every little sound hidden beneath its hum grows louder around me. Moving around the room, I close three sets of curtains, but the fourth set stops me in my tracks. They're already drawn. I don't remember doing that. I always open them in the morning. Always.

Reaching for the curtain, I hesitate before pulling the thick fabric tighter, trying to find an explanation. Maybe the cat was playing over here.

I drag myself to the kitchen, switching off the remaining lights, except for the entry, which I leave on for Hunter's return, then head upstairs. I'm guessing it's going to be another late one for him.

Fifteen minutes later, I lay awake, alone in this empty shell of a bed. The room surrounding me is an inky black, save for a few slivers of muted moonlight that sneak through the space where the curtains haven't quite met. With eyes wide, I stare into the abyss above, without focusing on anything in particular. Though the room feels different from earlier today. Less menacing, less foreboding. Just the desolate despair and loneliness that never dissipates.

Back to the familiar. Melancholy and alone. A warm tear forms in the corner of my eye, then falls, rolling down my cheek and onto the pillow. It's one of many, and I turn over onto my side, facing the ensuite.

Where is Hunter tonight? Is he really tied up in business, like he always claims? Or is someone else keeping his attention, feeding his desire? The thought twists in my chest, sharp and relentless. I've read about red flags like these before. The late nights, the secrecy. Any other woman would have seen it by now. Any *normal* woman. But am I even that anymore? Normal? Or have I become something smaller, someone more willing to ignore the truth to keep the pieces of this life intact?

None of which I will find answers for tonight.

Glancing at the alarm clock, it read 1 am. Squeezing my eyes closed again, as if wringing out the last of my pitiful sadness. And when there are no more tears left to spill, my heavy eyes fall to sleep.

Two hours later, the mattress dips beneath Hunter's weight, dragging me from a restless sleep. He shifts beside me, tugging at the comforter as he settles in. Feigning sleep, I keep my eyes shut and breath steady. Anything to keep him from noticing me

He doesn't bother me. After the day I've had, I just can't. Not tonight.

The mattress seems to jump a little. Then, the hair on the back of my neck prickles, as his whiskey-laden breath breathes heavily against the back of my neck. I want to yell at him, to cuss him out. Tell him to get away from me. To keep his grotty hands to himself. To go to his mistress instead... My heart pounds at each suggestion, almost willing me on. However, I'm not one to take chances. Don't be foolish, Marlys.

Hunter's hand wraps around my hips, rough and possessive, sliding between my legs as he presses hard against my back. I stiffen and hold on to safety for as many seconds as I can manage before surrendering to his ragged game of control. I can't fight it, or him. If I do, he'll just be getting more of what he wants.

Relenting from my rigid position, I soften like a ball of

clay, ready at his disposal, sending my mind off into another world. The old Hunter—the one I fell in love with—was a sweet romantic. He opened doors for me, and kissed the back of my hand, like I was the only woman in the world. Even his eyes spoke of his love and desire. Glistening whenever he caught my attention, ever so happy just to be in my mere presence. It's vastly different to now. Sometimes I wonder if I simply imagined that version of him.

"Good girl," he whispers in my ear in a low, menacing tone that makes all the hairs on my body stand on end. There's no need for me to speak. I'm just a toy for his pleasure. And at least if he gets what he wants tonight, he might wake in a good mood tomorrow.

When he finishes, sweat drips from his face and chest onto my bare back. He squeezes each of my hips, burning like fire before releasing me from his tenuous grasp. He flops onto the bed beside me, satisfied. I roll back onto my side, numb, yet the physical discomfort endures like it always does.

6

DINNER WITH THE DEVIL

MARLYS

Lack of sleep leaves my mind a foggy mess this morning. Climbing out of bed, I quickly shower and dress. Before the bathroom mirror, I hold my own gaze, practicing the smile I'll plaster on at breakfast. But the closer I peer into the depths of my irises, it's as if an entirely different person is reflecting back at me. It's unnerving, and my skin prickles. I splash water over my face, resetting my demeanour.

Behind me, Hunter stirs in bed. The pain from hours earlier, finally dissipating, yet the emotional toll remains.

How did things go from wonderful to... whatever this is, now?

Deep down, I know the answer, but I can't bring myself to acknowledge it. Not yet.

Racing downstairs to the kitchen, I prepare breakfast. Half an hour later, Hunter strolls into the adjoining dining room, fumbling with his tie.

"Good morning," I say, forcing out the words along with a sweet smile. "Coffee?"

He glances up at me, finally finished with his tie, but his smile doesn't reach his eyes. "Thanks."

Sliding into a chair, he pulls out his phone, reading something that makes his brows furrow unnaturally close together. I set down his breakfast before him, placing one hand on his shoulder to gain his attention. But he's fixated on the screen.

"Is everything alright?" I ask, trying to see what's captivating his interest.

He rips the phone away, shoving it into his jackets breast pocket. "What have I told you about reading over my shoulder?"

I take a small step backwards, retreating to a safe distance. He notices my unease and forcibly smooths out his expression.

"Sorry, I didn't mean to snap." He runs a hand through his pristine hair, ruffling it ungracefully. "I've got a lot on my mind right now. Some... *things* are not going as planned."

Smiling weakly, I don't say a word.

"Kage isn't up yet," he says, but it's more a question as to why I haven't ensured he's up and ready for school.

"Um, about that." I don't want to throw him under the bus. Rummaging through my mind, I find an acceptable excuse for his absence. "He's not well today."

"He's sick? He was fine yesterday," he says like he doesn't believe me.

Rising from his seat, he walks over to me standing on the other side of the kitchen island, and hands me his coffee cup. He leans in toward my cheek, dabbing a brief practised kiss, devoid of all emotion. I pass him his lunch, prepared earlier along with a note, smiling flawlessly.

"It's probably just a twenty-four-hour bug. Don't worry

about it, you have enough on your mind. I'll take care of him."

"Alright then," he says, turning away.

"Everything ready for the dinner party?" Hunter asks, but it feels like a challenge. One I'm now realising I've teetered very close to failing.

"That's tonight?" I ask, as my pulse begins to race. I can't believe I forgot about that, but I can't admit my faux pas to him, or else all hell will break loose. He watches me like his eyes are burrowing into my brain and reading my mind. My lip twitches, searching for an answer. "Of course. Everything is planned. I just need to grab a few things from the grocery store. Will you be home before the guests arrive?"

"Should be." He nods curtly. "Everything will be perfect?" His gaze shifts to a side table, then runs a finger over the top like he's expecting it to be filthy. Then huffs dismissively. "Right, Marlys?" I nod, despite the growing anxiety. "Good. And make sure Xander is here. I need his advice on something."

"Okay," I say. "Have a good day." But he's already out of earshot, in his office. It's that, or he's just being decidedly dismissive. Either could be true.

Through the glass panels of the office door, I watch him grab a messy stack of papers from his desk, stuffing them into his briefcase, before shooting towards the front door.

I suck in a deep breath as it slams behind him, unmoving until I hear his car leave. My shoulders fall, letting out a haggard sigh, now breathing easier. But then I spot something on the stairwell.

Kage stomps slowly down the stairs, rubbing his eyes. He ambles towards the kitchen, sliding into a chair at the table, slouching against the tabletop. After reheating his breakfast, I pull it from the microwave, placing it in front of him.

Little Liquorice meows, rubbing against his leg. He pushes her away, but she meows again like she's telling him off for his dismissal. Spinning around in a figure eight, she weaves through his legs before returning to her original position. Her head rubs against his hairy leg, but he doesn't shoe her away this time. Rather, a small smile creeps up the side of his face, as he pats his thigh, beckoning her to jump up.

She pounces onto his lap, instinctively rubbing against his chin. Watching him drop his guard like that is heartwarming. It's sweet and kind, and gives me hope that he won't turn out like his father. But then again, Hunter had groomed me too, hadn't he? Drawing me in, petting me just like this feline, until he'd gained all of my trust.

I choose hope for Kage, to see the beauty instead of the ugliness. He's capable of so much more. Perhaps he can be the man that his father couldn't be. Will never be. That maybe his mother's DNA might sway him to 'the good side' instead.

"Will you be alright if I pop next door for a few minutes?" I ask Kage. He's tearing apart his bacon, offering tiny portions to the feline in between his own mouthfuls.

"Of course," he scoffs. "Do you think Liquorice and I are going to throw a rave while you're gone?"

"Ok, I won't be long," I say, ignoring his sarcasm.

Maybe I should lock the door behind me? My hand rests on the doorknob, hesitating. It'll be fine for a few minutes, surely.

I head over to Xander's. Rapping my knuckles on the front door, he greets me, coffee in hand, breakfast radio playing in the background.

"Marlys. Hey," he says. He seems happy to see me, but there's also an ounce of surprise.

"Hey, Xander. I'm really sorry to disturb you so early," I say, glancing briefly at the mug in his hand. "I can come back later if you're still waking up."

"No, it's fine. Come in, I'll get you a cup." Waving a hand, he ushers me inside, but I shake my head apologetically.

"Actually, as much as I'd love to, I really don't have time today. I just came over to invite you to the dinner party tonight."

Xander rests against the door frame, crossing his ankles. "Dinner party, huh?"

"Please come," I say almost begging. "Hunter wants you there."

His eyebrows shoot high on his forehead. "He does, does he?"

I nod. "He said he might need your advice, but I don't know what about. A work thing, I think. He doesn't talk to me about that kind of thing, but I've noticed he's been stressed a lot more than usual lately." Xander's watchful gaze tells me I'm bumbling, and I force myself to quiet.

Rubbing his thumb and forefinger over his chin, he appears to consider the request. "For you, Marlys. I'll be there."

"Thanks, Xander. You're a lifesaver," I say, unable to hide my delight. "Anyway, I'd better get back—lots of prep still to do. I'll see you at seven."

Ticking the first task off my list, I set home, scanning the street as I walk. My skin prickles as if someone has eyes on me, burning into my skin. It's unsettling, especially so early in the morning. Nearing home, I note something sticking out of the letter box. The mailman hasn't come yet, I've never see him before lunch.

My stomach knots as I pull the envelope out. On the front, written in elegant, black cursive script, is the single word, 'Hunter'. A solid black line underlines his name with a full stop situated where the line ends. But the thing that sticks out the most is the lack of mailing or return address, and there's no postage stamp either. There's not a single clue that tells me who the sender is. An icy shiver runs up my spine as it occurs to me that the sender, whomever they are, must've been here. At our home. I scan the street again, still feeling uneasy. Yet nothing appears out of place.

Inside, the remnants of Kage's breakfast rest on the table, whilst he's spread out on the lounge, TV blaring. Perhaps I should try and talk to him about the school incident again? To figure out how to fix whatever mess he's gotten himself into. But then again, I have so much to do before tonight. Do I really have the time? The guilt eats at me, putting the dinner party preparations ahead of him. It feels wrong, and selfish, yet the truth is, he'd probably respond negatively, anyway. And then there would be Hunter to deal with, especially if dinner doesn't go off without a hitch.

Instead, I clean up from breakfast before putting together a menu for tonight. I set up the formal dining room for dinner, and after cleaning the rest of the ground floor, I head upstairs to get ready at six-thirty.

The doorbell chimes at six fifty-five, and I race downstairs to greet the first guest.

I straighten my knee length, figure-hugging black dress–the one that Hunter bought for the first corporate event we attended as a couple–then glancing in the mirror to ensure my make-up is on point. With poised posture, and perfected smile I open the door to greet the first guest.

But Xander stands before me.

My feigned smile changes to something more natural. I'm truly happy to see him. I know he'll help me get through this corporate drone of a dinner.

Letting out a sigh of relief, I take him by the elbow, ushering him inside. Guiding him through the entryway towards the lounge room where the guests will enjoy pre-dinner drinks.

"Thank goodness you got here first."

"You look stunning, Marlys," he says after scanning me top to toe. My face warms under his gaze.

The bar holds an impressive collection of top-tier liquor bottles, lined up like soldiers. "Thanks. What can I get you?"

"I'll take a scotch, if you have it." Pouring him his drink, I hand it to him. Swapping it for the bottle he arrived with. "A little something to go with dessert."

The label says it's a five-year-old, limited release Botrytis Semillon. "Sounds wonderful, thank you. Please, sit. Get comfy. I'll pop this in the fridge and be right back." With the wine in the refrigerator, I return to the lounge room and enjoy a glass of Moscato while we await for the remaining guests.

"How are things going, anyway?" Xander asks. He's referring to my respective relationships with Hunter and Kage, but now isn't the time for deep and meaningful conversation. Especially since Hunter will be home any minute.

"So, so," I reply, half-heartedly.

"I see." He pauses for a long moment, before changing the topic. "What have you cooked up for us tonight then?"

My answer is cut short by the sound of the front door opening. I spring to my feet and hurry to the door, worried that I didn't hear our guests arrive. But there are no guests, just Hunter. He studies me, frowning, then checks his watch.

"Has anyone arrived yet?" he asks impatiently.

"Just Xander," I say, tipping my head towards the lounge room. "Do you want to wash up first, or will you be joining him for a drink?"

He walks towards the lounge room, with me following behind, scurrying to catch up.

"I'll take a whiskey, thanks hun." The warmth of his words throws me off guard. It's been so long since we've been in public together, I'd almost forgotten what it's like.

In the armchair, he sits with one ankle resting on his knee. I hand him the whiskey; he responds in kind, briefly rubbing his hand on my lower back. He thanks me, raising my hand to his lips, and pressing a kiss against it. The sensation is a blurry mix of the old Hunter I once knew, the passion he had for me, but also dreadfully chilling, a reminder of what's hiding in plain sight.

I recall last night. It's only one night of many. An invisible album of memories I'd rather forget. My heart twists with ire, fuelling a sullen rage within. But now is not the time. Push it back down, Marlys.

"Xander, what are you doing for work at the moment?" He takes a long sip of his drink.

"Officially, I'm in early retirement, but I dabble in some consulting work from time to time."

Hunter jiggles his cup from side to side, ice clinking against the glass. "I might have some work for you, then."

It seems both men have forgotten I'm still in the room. But despite invisibility, I detect an odd look that passes between them, a shared understanding. I thought they were merely acquaintances–neighbours - not close friends, like this exchange would have me believe.

The doorbell rings again.

Hunter looks at me. "Marlys, do you mind getting that please?" Do I mind? Please? Those words seem foreign coming from him, but I play the part of devoted and obedient wife.

I greet a couple at the door. I can't say I remember meeting them before, but I usher them in, offering drinks once we reach the others.

Hunter places his glass on the table and stands, buttoning his jacket, before approaching the man. He pulls him into a half-hearted hug, patting him on the back three times before releasing him. There's a stiffness in the man's posture. He's not as thrilled to see Hunter as Hunter is to see him.

"Xander, you remember Grayson Whitmore?" Hunter announces, one arm still wrapped around the man.

"How could I forget? Grayson, it's been quite a while." Xander stands and proffers a brief handshake before turning to the woman by Grayson's side. He tilts his head slightly. "And you must be his better half?"

The woman elegantly holds out her hand. "Brielle Maddox. And no, we're not together, just business partners." Her voice is as silky smooth as the dress that flows from the thin straps on her shoulders, down to her ankles, where it meets her four-inch heels. She turns to face my husband, who holds her stare for an awkwardly long moment that makes me question how well the two of them know each other. But then his expression shifts back to the professional façade.

"Brielle, this is my wife, Marlys," he says, wrapping an

arm around my waist as if he owns me. And while the words sound friendly enough, it's almost as though he's giving her an unspoken warning.

She offers me a hand. Unlike when she greeted Hunter, her smile now displays a kindness that radiates from her eyes. Her voice is warm and gentle. "Marlys, it's so lovely to put a face to the name. Thank you for having us."

I return the smile. "It's my, uh, our pleasure," I say, bumbling over my words. Yet, I see Hunter give me a fleeting, reproving glance. Think before you speak, Marlys. "Can I get you both a drink before dinner?"

Fifteen minutes later, I usher the group into the formal dining room. Hunter sits at the head of the table, of course. My seat is to his left, but I remain standing as the others sit: Xander beside me, whilst Grayson sits opposite me to Hunter's right, and Brielle opposite Xander.

I hurry back to the kitchen, working quickly but with care I plate the entrees. Bringing two plates at a time, I serve Hunter first, then Grayson, followed by the other two guests on the next trip, before placing my own on the table.

Two bottles of wine rest beside the floral centrepiece— one red, and one white. I offer each guest their preference then take my seat.

Hunter raises his glass. "To successful business ventures."

The others raise their glasses, but Grayson doesn't smile. His lips draw into a tight line and his jaw clenches. Xander clinks his glass against mine, then offers it to clink against Grayson, while the others do the same before placing their glasses down.

I hope this entrée is to Hunter's liking, and that it goes down well with the others.

He takes his first bite, I hold my breath, teetering on the

edge of my seat. But then his forehead crinkles and nods in satisfaction. A sense of relief comes over me as I finally take a bite.

"This is just lovely Marlys," Brielle says. "Where did you learn to cook like this?"

I'm uncomfortable with the compliment, since I seldom get them. "I'm largely self-taught. Not having to work has its benefits, plenty of time to make a mess in the kitchen."

"Indeed," she says. "That will be a blessing for you when you have children."

Hunter clears his throat, interrupting the conversation. "Marlys doesn't want children. Besides, she's already got her hands full with Kage." But that isn't true at all. I do want children of my own–someday. Just not right now, and, maybe not even with Hunter. But he'd kill me if I admitted that out loud. No, that's a secret I'll keep to myself. One that even Xander doesn't know.

"Kage?" Brielle asks curiously.

"My stepson," I reply, gently. "Hunter's son from his first marriage."

"Oh, I see," she remarks, turning to Hunter. "I wasn't aware you'd been married before. Is this your second marriage then?"

He shifts uncomfortably in his seat. But then I catch him flashing Xander a quick panicked expression. "Yes, something like that."

Brielle looks at me with pity. "I read an article recently. It was quite interesting, but also very sad. Were you aware that the odds of a second marriage working out is even lower than the odds of a first marriage–which I think half end in divorce, so maybe half of that again, one in four are successful. Odds are even worse for third marriages." But then she lets out a bubbly laugh. "What do

I know, though? Those numbers are probably all skewed anyway."

"Anyway, enough of that," Hunter says, diverting the conversation. "We're here to talk business. Aren't we?"

Under the table, Xander pats my leg, reassuringly. Yet my mind is still reeling over those statistics. Did our marriage really start out having only a one in four chance of success? I wish I'd known that a year ago.

Grayson speaks in a low tone. "If we can strike a deal that works for everyone."

Brielle smiles, trying to ease the palpable tension. "We want to make sure the deal is fair *this* time."

"Exactly, and no underhanded tactics," Grayson adds, pulling his brows together.

Hunter leans back in his chair, swirling his glass. "Grayson, you know me better than that. Everything I do is above board."

Grayson's tight smile barely shifts, voice calm and measured. "That's not how I remember it."

Brielle reaches for her wine, her delicate fingers tracing the rim of the glass before lifting it. "Let's not dredge up the past," she says smoothly, her eyes hovering towards Hunter. "We all know how the business world works. What matters is moving forward."

Hunter points his fork at Brielle. "Of course. We're all on the same page here."

There it is again! That strange look between him and Brielle.

"Well Hunter, it's reassuring to know you're such an upstanding man." She turns to me. "You must be so proud of your husbands success. Business-savvy and handsomely charming."

I nod— not wanting to say anything that might add to

this tense exchange. Masking my unease, I smile broadly, standing from the table. "Please excuse me, the next course is ready."

Moving around the table, I gather the empty entrée dishes and head to the kitchen. My mind recoils to the strange glances at the table–the one between Hunter and Brielle, and towards Xander. It's curious being on the edge like this. Not knowing the truth of their shared histories. Knowing that you're the odd one out.

I stack the dishwasher, before serving the main meals atop the kitchen island, concentrating intently. When it's done, I take a step back, double checking that I've plated it to perfection. That's what's expected, after all. I pick up two of the plates, balancing precariously.

"Need a hand?" Xander offers, unexpectedly rounding the corner.

Skittery, I jump, both plates overbalancing in my hands. One falls to the floor in a sloppy hot mess of pasta, but Xander rushes forward, saving the other. I'd been so into my thoughts I hadn't even noticed him enter the room.

"Oh, my goodness, look at this mess," I say, scanning the splatter. Tears well in my eyes, as I gather the mess in paper towels. Xander crouches to my position on the floor, resting a hand on my wrist.

"Let me," he says kindly, "It's my fault after all." But I shake my head.

"You're a guest, you shouldn't be cleaning up. You shouldn't even be in here," I say.

Grabbing the paper towel from my hands, he proceeds to clean up. "Don't be ridiculous, Marlys. We're neighbours–friends–there's no need for formalities with me."

"Fine," I huff, but I appreciate the help.

Replacing the lost meal, I garner the extra portions and ready the other plate. A minute later Xander follows me into the formal dining room, serving up the meals.

"Everything Okay in there?" Hunter asks.

I wave his concern off, worrying the truth might dampen his reasonably good mood. "It was nothing. Just a little accident, it's all sorted out now."

The conversation through the main meal is more light-hearted than before, but it's almost as if it's a mask. Is that for my benefit? I'm not sure. I serve crème brûlée for dessert along with the wine Xander had brought with him, without further incident and I suspect the evening went about as well as Hunter could have hoped for. When all is said and done, I take Hunter's arm, following the guests to the front door.

"Thank you again, Marlys, for a wonderful evening. Perhaps we can do it again sometime," Brielle says, brushing her hand against my upper arm.

I nod. "That sounds lovely."

Hunter and Grayson share a few whispered words as Brielle, and I exchange contact details. Watching them head back to their car, I close the door. I turn to Hunter, but he's already gone. I find him in the lounge room, another whiskey in hand, tapping out something on his phone. His concerned expression is evident as he concentrates on whatever, and whomever, he's messaging.

When he's done, he squares it away, back in his jacket pocket. Placing his cup on the table beside him, he stands, finally noticing me in the room.

"Are you going somewhere?" I ask, as he buttons his jacket.

"I need to see Xander," he says matter-of-factly.

"What? Now? It's late." I glance at the wall clock above the television.

"Don't wait up." He brushes past me, but then pauses for a second, taking a step backwards to stand in front of me. I hold his stare, heart pounding not knowing what's going through his head. Then his expression changes. For the briefest of moments, I see the old Hunter. The kind, loving one, that would do anything for me. He raises his hand to my cheek. I flinch, but he makes contact. It's gentle, and warm. Confusion spreads through my mind and body. Then in one swift move, he brushes his lips against mine, tender and passionate. And I almost forget about all the toxic in our relationship. As fast as it began, it ends, and Hunter heads out the door.

A short while later, laying in bed under the comforter, my mind replays the nights events in sharp fragmented moments. Grayson's clenched jaw, Brielle's too-bright smile, and the lingering glances that passed over the table, like I wasn't even there. And the confusing kiss from Hunter.

Then there was the envelope with elegant script spelling out his name. I didn't tell him about it, but maybe I should have.

7

WHAT ISN'T THERE

MARLYS

Even before I open my eyes, the air is thick with suffocating oppression. It wasn't like this when I went to bed last night. It's familiarity like an unsettling memory that claws in my mind. My body stiffens under the covers, and I squeeze my eyes shut tighter, willing myself not to notice. But the smothering quiet is inescapable, blending with a heaviness that makes it hard to breathe.

My hand shuffles, creeping along the fitted sheet straining for Hunter's warmth. The silky-smooth Egyptian cotton sheets don't falter under my fingertips. Even the crisply tucked top sheet remains intact, taught against its secure hold beneath the mattress. There's no creases, no crumbs, nothing at all. Just the subtle chill of untouched bedding. Where is he?

I roll onto my side. A cool breeze tickles the exposed skin on my back, where my nightdress's thin satin fabric doesn't cover. Shivering, I resist the urge to burrow deeper under the covers. I peek one eye open, so slightly that it could easily go unseen. Blurry eyed at first, I focus on the other side of the bed. To the vacant space beside me, where my husband should be.

The confirmation of his absence fuels my racing pulse. Did he really see Xander last night? Or was it just a faintly veiled ruse to get me off his back? Maybe he was with Brielle? Things seemed off last night, and I know I witnessed strange glances between them. I suspected he was having an affair, all those little red flags I'd noticed–late nights, whispered calls, the new cologne he'd bought himself. It all adds up, doesn't it?

How can he do this to me? Our marriage is barely a year old. I'm still the same person he met. Or at least, I think so. Anger burns, daring flames to leap from my skin. Just the thought of his betrayal makes me feel like my whole body is turning inside out. How dare he?

Getting out of bed, I don't bother getting dressed. I throw my dressing gown on, tying at the waist tightly. Down the hallway, I crack open the door to Kage's bedroom. He's still fast asleep. It's the weekend so I leave him be.

Once I head down the stairs, I check the lounge room. On rare occasions he falls asleep in the chair, whiskey still in his hand. Another red flag, I realise. But I can't think about that now. Checking his office and the kitchen, little Liquorice breaks the silence with a tentative meow.

"Not now," I scold her.

She follows me to the front door, where I pull aside a curtain. Hunter's car is parked in the driveway. He must be here. I let out a deep breath, perhaps he wasn't with her last night then. But where is he? Surely, he's not still at Xanders?

Maybe I should call Hunter and see where he is. But if he is with her... I don't want to think about that. I can't.

Pushing the pain aside, I grab my phone, scrolling through my recent calls until his name flashes on the screen. My thumb hovers above, hesitating. Do I really want to know the answer to my question? My heart thuds inside my chest. Yes, I need to know. I select call and press the phone to my ear.

It rings.

And rings.

Until finally it goes to voicemail. Hanging up without leaving a message, my pulse rises, faster and more furious. What the actual fuck Hunter?

I try again, rapping my painted nails against the kitchen counter. But still there's no answer.

Sucking in a deep breath, I try to steady my nerves, but it doesn't help. Flicking back to my recent calls, I search for Xanders name and call. He picks up on the third ring.

"Hey Marlys," he says, but the warmth in his voice doesn't register against the vicious thoughts swirling in my head.

"Is Hunter there?" The words rush out, louder and more earnest than I'd meant.

"Um, no. Should he be?"

"He went to see you last night. After the dinner party."

"Yeah." Xanders voice quivers ever so slightly. Silence falls on the other end of the phone, for just a few seconds. Then his voice returns, clearing his throat before speaking. "What's going on?"

My eyes begin to blur, wet from the welling tears, and my voice catches in my throat. "He never came home last night."

Xanders voice drops, and my stomach sinks along with it. "Oh."

A long silence on the other end makes me check my

phone. The call is still connected. I press it back to my ear. "Xander?"

"Uh, yeah, sorry Marlys. I was just thinking," he says. "I'll be right there. Give me two minutes, alright?"

I nod my head as if he can see through the phone. "Thanks."

Staring at the blank screen, my mind reels with what's happening. This can't be real. This is something that happens to other people, not to me. But it is, isn't it?

Returning to my recent calls, I try Hunter again. And again, it goes to voicemail. This time I decide to leave a message. "Hunter, it's me." My voice shakes despite my best efforts to sound chirpy. "I'm just wondering where you are. Give me a call back as soon as you can." I search for what else to say. What would a good wife say in this moment? To make her husband return? "I love you." I'm not sure whether it's love, or concern, or some other strange emotion that I'm feeling right now. But if anything is going to make him call me, to come home, perhaps that will help. Besides, it's not as if I never loved him.

I shake my head, rattling my reverie, but it's interrupted by knocking at the front door.

Once I let Xander in, he stands before me, brows pulled together tightly. Then he brings me into his chest, rubbing the length of my back, reassuringly.

"Shh," he says, over my muffled sobs that I know will leave a pool of tears on his shirt. But that's the furthest thing from my mind right now.

When he releases me from the embrace, still standing inches apart, he glances down at me with pity. Raising one hand, he brushes away the tears with his thumb. "Come on, let's get you some coffee. It'll help you think more clearly."

I follow him to the kitchen, heading for the kettle, but he waves me away. "Sit, please. Let me get this for you," he says with a kindness only Xander can manage.

Taking a seat at the table, my gaze wanders to the large window on the other side of the room. Staring into the nether, the trees and bushes distort into shades of green and brown, dotted with flowering pinks and yellows around the garden. It's a mix of indistinct shapes, slightly wavering with the breeze. From the corner of my eye, a hazy figure appears. Drawing me in, I shift, focussing on the area. Could it be Hunter? No, a trick of the mind, or shade thrown by clouds moving overhead.

Xander places a cup of coffee in front of me, rubbing my back briefly, before taking the seat opposite. He observes me closely while I take a long sip, closing my eyes in a desperate attempt to reset my head space. When I open them again, nothing has changed. I sigh, shoulders slumping involuntarily.

"Better?" he asks.

"A little," I say.

"Let's start from the beginning." He keeps his voice low and tentative as if I might break.

I explain how I woke this morning. How Hunter's side of the bed remains undisturbed. How I tried to call him without success.

"And the last time you saw him?"

"When he went to see you," I confirm. "What time did he leave?"

"Around 2 am, give or take half an hour. I wasn't really keeping an eye on the time."

I watch him curiously. "What did he want to talk to you about anyway?"

He looks past me, towards the lounge room. "Just work stuff."

I groan. "Hunter told me that much already." A growl emits from my throat. "He never tells me anything about work. The closest thing I've gotten to anything on the topic was hosting the dinner party last night. And even then, everything they mentioned went over the top of my head. Please, Xander. Don't treat me like I'm stupid. Just tell me what's going on." My eyes fall to my bundled hands, wringing atop the table. "Is something going on with Brielle?" I whisper, sorrowfully.

He stretches his hand across the table, meeting mine, giving it a gentle squeeze. "As far as I know, things between Hunter and Brielle are all business. He just wanted me to review something for his portfolio, to see if the numbers made sense–and if it's a wise investment, and has potential growth. That's all I know. I'm sorry for whatever is going on. I wish there was more to tell you, I really do."

"I don't know. My gut says something is off. And even if he's not with her–not having an affair–I still don't know where he is. Should I try to find him, or maybe report him as missing to the police?"

"No," he blurts, shifting in his chair. "I'm sure there's a reasonable explanation. Just give it some time."

I scan his face, trying to see if there's something he's not telling me. Anything that might give a clue to his whereabouts. But he just gives a small smile, as if trying to lighten the moment.

"You're right, Xander. He'll call soon."

He nods, picking up his cup again.

Liquorice appears at my ankle, rubbing against it as she let's out a meow. Reaching down, I scratch the top of her head. Her purr vibrates through my fingertips, and I pick her up. She rubs against my cheek.

"Come on, let's get you some breakfast," I say, carrying her into the kitchen. I set her down beside her water bowl, before fetching the cat biscuits from the cupboard, filling her bowl. She doesn't notice the piece of our family that's missing. But then again, he's never been much of an animal person.

Returning to the table, I settle in my seat, and pick up my half-empty cup, sipping. I stare past Xander, to the window, unfocussed. Just thinking.

"Oh my God, Xander." My words rush out as I grab my phone, and scrolling through the contacts. "Brielle, she gave me her number last night." Glancing up, seeking permission that I don't actually need, to call her.

He checks his watch. "It's a bit early still, but if it'll ease your mind, then, why not?"

Pressing call, I put the phone on speaker so both of us can hear. It rings a few times, before a woman's voice answers.

"Hello?" she says, sleepily.

I cross my arms on the table, leaning towards the phone. "Brielle?" I ask, eyes locked on Xander as I speak.

"This is she."

Sighing, my stomach does a little summersault. If she was with Hunter, she wouldn't answer my call, right?

"Brielle, it's Marlys," I say.

She perks up on the other end. "Oh, hey Marlys. I wasn't expecting your call so early."

"I know, I'm sorry if I woke you."

"It's fine, I'm up now. What can I do for you?"

Hesitating, my mind searches for the right words. I let out a weak laugh. "This is going to sound silly, but I was just wondering if you heard from Hunter after dinner last night?" I pause before adding. "Or saw him?"

Brielle's voice wavers like I've caught her off guard. But then again, if she's reading between the lines, maybe I've just insulted her. But the need to know my husband's location is more important than worrying about whether I have pissed her off.

"Uh, no, sorry Marlys. I haven't spoken with him or seen him since we left your place last night." Her voice lowers, "Is everything alright?"

Trying to mask my worry, I force a smile as I speak. "It's probably nothing. I'm sorry to have bothered you. I'll let you get back to sleep, or..." My words trail off.

Ending the call, the phone sits squarely on the table between us.

One side of Xander's mouth pulls into a half smile. "Well, I think that answers one of your questions, doesn't it?"

"I suppose so," I reply.

"Could you try the office number?" he suggests.

I shake my head. "No, there'll be no one there on the weekend. It just goes to the office voicemail."

"Right, I forgot about that."

"What about Grayson? Could he have gone to see him?"

"I doubt it. They're not close like that," he says, pulling his brows together.

"What do you mean?" I ask curiously.

His jaw clenches, and mouth draws into a tight line. "I don't want to speak out of turn." Observing him closely as he thinks, I can see the cogs turning in his mind. "A long time ago, before you met Hunter, they were practically inseparable. Best friends, if you will."

"Really?" I say, flabbergasted. "I would never have guessed that. What happened?"

"Things went south over a business deal if I remember correctly. If I'm being honest, I was surprised to see him here last night."

"He didn't mention anything to me either. Do you think Grayson could have anything to do with Hunter not coming home?"

"I don't see how he would. Like I said, their relationship is only business, and from last night, I don't think Grayson is happy about the deal—or maybe it's simply that the deal is with Hunter. Either way, I really don't think it has anything to do with this current issue."

Slumping in my seat, I take a breath before sighing it out slowly. If only Hunter had told me more about his life outside of these walls, then I'd have some idea where to start looking for him. But he didn't, and I wonder if he orchestrated it that way. To keep his personal and professional lives apart.

"What about his parents?" I say.

"What about them?" Xanders asks intriguingly.

"Could he have gone there?"

He glances down at the table, shaking his head. "There's more chance he'd call Grayson."

"Well, I'm all out of ideas. The only other thing I can think of is to go drive around looking for him, but that seems rather pointless."

"I'm not sure what else to do either, Marlys," he says.

"What if something really bad has happened to him? Are you sure I shouldn't just call the police? They could probably do that thing I've seen on TV where they track his phone—what do they call it? Triangulate his location from the phone towers, or whatever."

Xander laughs. "You watch far too many crime channels. But seriously, missing persons cases tend to be children, or vulnerable women, or elderly. I can't say I've ever heard of a missing persons case that involved a CEO of a successful business."

He makes a good point. Whenever I've watched shows about missing people, it's always some woman from a bad relationship, or a child caught in the middle of a broken family. And then there are those who've fallen on hard times, and fell in with a bad crowd–drugs, drinking, sex work, and things like that. None of that resembles Hunters life–at least the parts that I know about.

"All we can do is wait," Xander says, reaching across the table. He pats the back of my hand gently and his voice lowers. "I'm sure you'll hear from him soon."

"Thanks, " I say, but I'm not convinced.

A few minutes later, I send him home. There's nothing either of us can do right now, I'll just have to try and be patient.

Kage wakes, and heads downstairs for breakfast. But amidst all the chaos, I didn't prepare anything this morning.

"It's fine," Kage grumbles. "I'll just Uber something."

When the driver arrives twenty minutes later, I call out to him, but he doesn't appear. Probably has his head in the clouds, music blaring through his headphones again. I head outside, to meet the delivery guy, taking the brown paper bag. But then I notice something odd over on the footpath. After the driver leaves, I move towards it, never taking my eyes off it.

As I get closer, it comes into focus. Someone's wallet, still closed, sits in the middle of the concrete path. The dark brown leather looks familiar. My stomach sinks, bending to retrieve it.

With trembling fingers, I hold my breath as I unlatch the tiny clip fastening it together. Slowly it unfolds. A variety of cards sit amongst the slots on one side, but on the other, through the clear plastic film, sits a driver's licence.

The photo is old but unmistakable, the name even more so—Hunter Brannigan.

8

———————

NEED TO KNOW

MIRANDA

She saw me. I know she did. Her head turned, eyes squinting as they focused past Xander, through the window, and into the garden.

She's quick, but not as quick as me.

Camouflaged by the shrubbery, I disappear before she can be certain. Another close shave.

I don't know how long I've been out here this time. Even after he left, I stayed. I had to. Kage was there, after all. He's the reason I keep coming back. Well, that and the truth. If it's ever revealed. Vengeance, that might be enough to satisfy me.

Even from the other side of the windowpane, I sense something amiss. It's agonising, not knowing. Always an outsider, looking in. Construing every little, obscure detail, trying to discover its meaning. And who knows if I'm right? My instinct has proven spot-on before. It's a shame I wasn't more in sync with it when I was still with Hunter.

Scrutinising Marlys' movements, she returns to the table with something in her hand. Today, she must've been in a hurry when she did her hair. The uneven, messy gathering of blonde, with loose, erratic strands dangle from all sides. Even her face has an usual reddish hue to it, blotchy and unflattering. I can't imagine Hunter will be thrilled to see this hot mess. Although I haven't seen him today.

Slumped over the table, face buried beneath her hands, her shoulders shake, jarring forward, as tears spill from between her fingers. She's crying, really? Marlys' chest heaves as her sobs grow louder, no longer merely visceral. This heightened level of emotion is one I haven't seen before. Raw in all its forms. It only spurs my urgency to discover the cause.

Eventually, the ocean of tears withers away. She rises from her seat, brushing away the remains as she moves towards the kitchen, grabbing a box of white tissues to blow her nose. She tosses the used tissue into the bin and clutches the box as if it were her only hope. It all seems a bit melodramatic. But I suppose the younger you are, the harder life hits you. Still, the urge to slap her out of her self-pity remains.

I can't take my eyes off her. Drawn to her in her weakest moment. Though I don't pity her. What is she so worked up about? It's irritating, like a rash from the summer grass, relentlessly itchy no matter how hard you scratch, no matter how deep you push your fingernails into your skin, leaving trails of open flesh in their wake.

That's Marlys. The endless itch under my skin.

She ambles to the lounge room. From here, she's barely visible, sunken into the couch.

I need to get inside that house.

I need to know what's going on.

Leaving my post, I skirt around the perimeter to the back of the house, towards the patio and swimming pool.

The laundry room sits behind the kitchen. Sometimes she forgets to lock that door. I scan the garden and neighbouring yards for privacy. Xander is just metres away. He isn't looking here, but that doesn't mean he won't. No, I can't hang around here too long.

When he turns, I move, rounding the corner of the house, onto the patio. The guest bedroom, that sits behind the laundry room, has French doors that swing open to a pool view, while the other is a sliding double door that opens from the rumpus room. It appears no one has used either room recently. Everything is in its place like a show home, only a little more dated.

When I lived here, we were always in the rumpus room. I had an entire play area set up for Kage with all his little baby toys. I'd lay his blue blanket, embroidered with his name, down on the floor, and lay him on his back. He'd reach his tiny fingers up towards the dangling miniature safari creatures. The elephant being his favourite. And when it was my turn to host the mother's group, the others would park their little ones alongside him, while we relaxed on the couches with coffee and tea, watching them play while we chatted about everything in our lives.

I wonder if Kage still sees those children at school. Whether they've remained friends after all these years. I worry about him and how much my absence from has affected him.

The rumpus door is locked. Maybe with the key. I head back to the French doors of the guest room. They rattle as a breeze whips through the patio, shaking them on their hinges. It won't take much to pry these open. With intense focus, I fumble with the mechanism. It eventually gives way, doors breaking free as they squeal open. I freeze, listening for any clue that Marlys has heard the intrusion.

No footsteps or voices head this way. Scanning the yard, I slip inside, pulling the doors closed behind me, latching them securely. I creep further into the room, tiptoeing over the carpet.

When I reach the door to the hallway, I pause, trying to hear anything. But still, there's nothing. Ever so slowly, I turn the handle, moving into the hallway. Pressing my back against the wall, I inch my way towards the lounge room. Still, she doesn't seem to notice. I dare myself to keep moving, remaining hidden by the hall's shadows.

Curled up on the couch, Marlys stares at something in her hand, sobbing. Her hands and the distance prevent me from seeing what it is. Although she's whispering, I can't determine whether she's speaking to herself or the object. Either way, it borders on disturbing. Has she finally lost the plot, once and for all?

Vibrating comes from the coffee table and her sobs quieten, to a muted silence that encompasses the vast room. For a moment, it's so still that my ears ring. She reaches for her phone, pulling it towards her. Marlys' gasp slices through the stillness like a sharpened blade as she stares at the screen.

"Hunter?" she whispers, still staring at the screen, and just loud enough that I can hear her.

I strain to see what's happening, but it's a futile endeavour. Searching for a way to get closer without her noticing, I peer around for any suggestion. My efforts are in vain since the end of the hallway reveals the large open space of the lounge room floor. Damn it. I have no other choice than to stay put. At least for now.

Her brows furrow together, tipping her head to the side like she doesn't know what to make of what she's seeing. "What the hell?" she whispers again.

Examining the room again, I seek any options I might've missed before. My gaze lands on a photograph. The one of Kage I saw the other day. His face is distracting and I can't seem to pull myself away from him. The longer I stare, the more my heart aches, yearning for my son. Anger surges within, growing alongside my pain, fuelling the vengeance I crave—for ripping that away from me.

The photograph teeters on the edge of the side table, daring to overbalance. Then, in an instant, it crashes to the floor. There must've been a gust of wind I hadn't noticed. But it doesn't rightly matter now.

My eyes dart towards Marlys, whose attention shifts to the disturbance. She stands, her movements slow and deliberate as she warily approaches the side table. If she reaches it, there's a good chance she'll find me. I need to hide.

I retreat into the darkest shadows of the hallway, past the formal dining room, towards the rumpus room, and wait.

Reaching the table, she crouches to the floor, picking up the photograph in one hand. With the other, she places her phone inside her shirt before wiping her hand over the glass. Standing, she returns Kage's photo to its original spot alongside the scattering of other photos. She stares at the pictures, then picks up a different one and studies it.

"Where are you really?" she whispers again, then shakes her head. Marlys places it back on the table and retrieves her phone. Lifting it to her ear, she waits a moment, then speaks.

"Xander," she says, urgently. "I got a text."

She goes quiet again, then nods. "Yeah, but the wording... it doesn't sound like him. Something's off."

She listens again, then speaks with more urgency. "I know, but... my gut says it's not him."

Him? Is she referring to Hunter? Or worse, has something happened to Kage?

Marlys' voice breaks my train of thought, wavering as she speaks. "But Xander, if it's not him, who is it?"

9

THREE DAYS GONE
KAGE

School sucks more than being suspended. Slouched in the back row, I push my left ear bud further in, trying to blur out the chatter from the others at the adjacent desks. My right ear remains free, so it appears I'm paying attention.

"His dad's probably run off with his girlfriend," one girl whispers. But it isn't enough to stop me from hearing her.

"I'm not surprised, really," says the girl beside her. "He's freaking weird. That's why he has no friends."

My pulse rages with all the things I want to yell. Shut up! Mind their own business! But Marlys's words reverberate in my mind. I can't afford to get suspended again. Next time, I'll probably be expelled. She'd threatened home schooling as if the little time I already spend in her presence isn't enough.

Fuck no.

But as much as my step-mother grates on me, these callous wretches at school make me want to quieten them once and for all. Besides, what the fuck do they actually know. That BS about Dad having a girlfriend is gossip.

God knows his life revolves around his job. His one true love.

Everyone thinks I should be proud of him. To have achieved so much with his business. Able to afford the 'finer things in life'. At least that's what I'd overheard the other parents say at school pick up.

What exactly are 'the finer things' though?

The wine they buy for pretentious dinner parties, setting them back a few hundred bucks? Or his brand name business suits that cost as much as some teenagers' cars? Or perhaps it all depends on how big your parent's house is?

None of that shit matters.

I'd trade it all in to have a normal family. A mum who loves me, a dad who gives a shit, a sibling so I'm not all alone. And maybe a dog. That'd be nice. For now, I guess I should be thankful I have Liquorice. She seems to love me, even if she can't chase a ball.

Still, if I can't have a sibling, maybe they'll finally let me have a dog. I have to get him in a good mood first. He'll probably say 'yes' just to be done with the conversation.

Speaking of him, when will Dad be back?

Before I have a chance to consider the question, from the corner of my eye, I see the 'mean girls' turn to face me. Their hands cover their mouths, clearly whispering more bullshit about me, or my Dad, or who the fuck knows?

I squeeze my eyes closed, trying to refocus, to calm the fury still bubbling under the surface.

Don't bite back. Stay out of trouble.

I have to be smart. Bide my time.

A loud thwack comes from the front as the teacher leans over her desk. With her fists balled, she glares at the girls.

That bitch, Karma, finally caught up with them, huh? I thought it was made up by adults, trying to coax kids into behaving, but maybe there's truth to it. Problem is, if it's real, not just some made-up story like Santa Claus, I have consequences coming my way too.

But there are people who've done far worse than me. Surely, karma prioritises people like that.

When the school bell rings at the end of the day, I hang back as the room empties, avoiding any further opportunities for trouble. Finally, I can escape these four walls. But going home is like moving from one prison to another. There's always someone looking over my shoulder. Always someone with an opinion. What I should do, and how I should do it. Who I should do it with.

What the fuck do they know?

Fuck.

I want to scream. To empty my lungs of all the air, free myself from everything that suppresses me from being myself. But I wasn't raised that way.

Hold it in. Wait.

But how long do I wait? Forever?

Surely, there's a point where it's time to take action.

Trailing behind the other kids, a tap from a pointy finger jabs my shoulder. I turn to find the teacher standing there.

What could she possibly want now? I've already spent the best part of eight hours listening to numerous teachers drone on, about one thing or another.

Just let me leave already.

"Kage," she says. Her eyes are full of pity when she looks at me.

"Yeah," I huff impatiently, fidgeting with my ear bud.

"I wanted to check in with you. How are things at home?"

"Fine," I scowl. I hate being caught off guard like this,

but more importantly, why does she even think it's appropriate to talk in the damn classroom? She doesn't expect me to randomly open up to her, surely. Not here. Not anywhere, for that matter.

Her brows knit together, and she tilts her head, scrutinising me. "Hmm," she says, then pauses for a moment. Her voice is gentle, like I could break if she's too abrasive. "I overheard what those girls were saying." She watches me for a reaction, but I give her nothing in return. Besides, my family is none of her damn business. Her brows rise far on her forehead and she lets out a sigh. "Well then, if you need help with anything, please talk to me. Okay?" She raises a hand to pat the side of my arm, but I shrug her away.

"Can I go now?"

"Sure."

Pushing the other earbud into my ear, I crank up the volume, gaze fixed on the concrete path before me, but I know they're staring. All of them. I could chance a sideways glance, but it would just fuel my rage that I've managed to keep at a simmer.

Turning the corner, I remain focused, walking faster so I can get out of here. Away from the prying eyes. It's a disconcerting violation of privacy, like being naked.

At home, it's the same. Like someone is always standing over my shoulder. Always watching me. Everything I do, and everywhere I go. I know it's stupid, and maybe I'm broken and pathetic, like they say. Why else would Marlys nag me about therapy so often? As if telling a stranger my deepest thoughts might cure me from... well, my life. What a joke.

Rounding the corner, I pick up pace, heading for the lockers. When I get there, I spin the dial, flipping open the rectangular aluminium door. Grabbing my bag, I shove books, pens, and my lunch box in, before zipping it up and throwing it over my shoulder.

I'm out of here.

With the same brisk pace, I dart towards the school gates, scanning the road for Marlys's car. But she's not there. What the hell? She's always there, one of those helicopter parents as seen on the TV. Could I have missed her? Shuffling down the footpath, I strain, searching the row of cars for hers. Nope, she's definitely not here.

Pulling out my phone, I tap out a message begrudgingly. Initiating contact with her rubs me the wrong way since she gets a kick out of things like that. Se misconstrues it to mean I give a damn, or that I like her. I don't.

It's not that she's a bad person. She's just not mine. Dad chose her, brought her into our lives, without even considering how I feel about it. A nanny would've done. It's how we lived for years before they got hitched. It's like she's always trying to be my mother and I hate that. What's worse is when she tries to be my friend. Hard pass on that too. All the little things she does, the post it notes in my lunch, what's the point of it really?

My phone buzzes with a text from Marlys.

MARLYS

Running late. Sorry.

For fuck's sake, Marlys? On my first day back? Really? As if coming back to school after the suspension wasn't hard enough.

I punch out a reply, telling her not to bother. That I'll walk home instead. And to be honest, I'm not in any rush to get there. What's there to look forward to? The awkwardness between her and I that never changes, or the fact Dad's always working. Even when he's home, he's in that freaking office of his. If it weren't for the glass squares on the door, I wouldn't even know he was home.

She replies with another wordy text full of her usual bullshit. I send another, confirming not to come, then pack it back in my pocket.

When I get to the crossroad, I press the round metal button, waiting for the traffic to ease before darting across the road. Two more blocks pass, and I reach the field where I used to play soccer. I make a beeline for the concrete tables and benches, throwing my bag on the table when I reach it, I lay on the long hard seat. Bending my knees, I bring my hands behind my head and just be.

The concrete is cool against my back, and a light breeze licks my skin, but the sensation of being watched has finally gone. It might seem like nothing, but to me, it's like freedom: from school, home, prying eyes, expectations, from everything. But I can't stay here forever.

My mind drifts back to Marlys and Dad. And then to my mum. I hate that I can barely remember her. All I have are a few photos, hidden in my desk. Dad would kill me if he knew I had them. On the rare occasion, when I was little, if I asked him anything about her, he would lose it. She was completely off topic. Eventually, I learned not to ask.

I only found those photos by chance, playing 'Hide and seek'. Hidden underneath the stairwell, in a dark space filled with boxes.

I wish I knew what really happened between them, but more than that, I wish I knew why she had to leave me. I mean, I get it, Dad can be an asshole.

But she could have taken me with her. Couldn't she?

Occasionally I dream about her, doing Mum things with me like hanging out and talking about my day, or watching a movie and sharing a bowl of popcorn, or splashing each other playing Marco Polo in the pool. I love those dreams, little snippets of the life we could've had, and the family we could've been.

We didn't have to include Dad.

It could've been just her and I.

That would've been enough. But those dreams, sometimes they aren't so good. Every now and then, I have one that starts the same way, but then, when I'm looking at her, her face twists and shifts into a different woman. A woman that I've seen before, or at least I think I have.

I would never tell Dad about those dreams. God, no.

It's been three days since I saw him. Since their dinner party, where I was banished to my room. Marlys has been beside herself with worry, and I've overheard her conversations with Xander. How she wanted to call the cops. That seems a bit extreme. Yet, she tells me nothing. As if the gossip in this neighbourhood wouldn't get back to me. Ridiculous.

Not that I care. Why should I? I can't remember the last time he bothered talking to me like a human being, rather than some bratty fuck up of a kid. I know that's what he thinks of me.

Fuck him.

Even if I have to live with Marlys 'til I'm old enough to leave—I shudder at the thought—I'd rather do that than have him return. He can keep his stupid girlfriend, or whoever the fuck is keeping his attention. He clearly doesn't give a shit about me—or Marlys, for that matter.

We're better off without him. At least I am. But is that just another lie I've learned to live with? I'm not so sure anymore.

10

TO DISMISS AND DEFLECT
MARLYS

For three days, thoughts of Hunter and where he might be overrun my mind like wild ivy, creeping and winding through every dark crevice.

Living like this is anything but. Lack of sleep now clouds my mind, leaving me to question—the shadows, the stares, and the ominous truth about Hunter.

I should've heard from him by now.

Even mundane tasks challenge me, unable to simply do the dishes without incident. Fingers now wrapped in Band-Aids where knives sliced my flesh open, infecting the crockery with a red hue, infiltrating the once clear water until there's nothing left but the infestation.

The only thing left to do now is go to the police.

From the driver's seat of my car, the engine rumbles, my eyes fixed on the concrete façade before me. Vision glazing over the longer I stare, blurring from the edges into nothingness. Procrastinating only spurs my nerves on.

Get it together, already.

Closing my eyes, I suck in a deep breath, readying

myself to enter. I brush my sweaty palms against my jeans and grab my handbag. Inching the car door open, I slide out, standing in the gap for just a moment, fingers curling tightly around the door frame.

Shoving the door closed, I take two steps forward. Halting in my tracks, two police officers barge past me like I'm not even here. They dart through the automatic doors, I quickly scan my surroundings, ensuring no more misadventures, before dragging myself towards the entry.

Inside, the police station is much quieter than expected. An older woman sits at the reception desk, behind a glass panel. There's only a ten-centimetre gap at the bottom, with a circle of holes drilled in the centre for speaking through.

With my pulse racing ever faster, I approach the desk. The woman is focussed on her computer screen as she types frantically on the keyboard, not noticing my presence.

"Excuse me," I say.

She glances up, over the top of her black-framed glasses, taking me in. "How can I help you today?" Sitting up straighter in her chair, her body shifts to face me fully.

"I, uh, may I speak with someone about my husband?" The car keys I had forgotten I was still holding, slip from my left hand as my palms. Flashing her a brief forced smile, I crouch, picking them up and stashing them in my bag, before standing again. "Sorry," I whisper.

With a sympathetic smile, she questions me further. "Is this a DV matter?"

"DV?" I ask, not familiar with the term.

"Domestic violence. Do you need a protection order?"

"Oh, no," I say, surprised at the realisation. "My husband, well, I think he's missing."

Her brows knit together. "You *think* he's missing?" she repeats.

I nod. "He left home on Friday night and I haven't heard from him since."

"Have you tried calling him?" she asks.

What the heck? This woman must think I'm stupid. Maybe I made a huge mistake coming here. I would've been better off finding a private detective.

"His phone is switched off. I've tried everyone I could think of. I can't find him. And..." My gaze falls to my fingers, nervously pulling at a hangnail. "I don't know what else to do."

She stands from her seat, eying me again. "If you don't mind waiting, you can take a seat over there." She waves to a row of chairs.

The woman disappears through a door in the back of the room as I sit and wait. The quietude is almost suffocating, observing posters and flyers around the space warning of locking cars to prevent theft, family violence awareness, and an array of other civic duties.

As I wait, my mind recoils back to Hunter. Has something dreadful happened to him, or is he just doing this to be selfish? What if someone kidnapped him like in the movies? He has money. The idea isn't as farfetched as it sounds, right? But even I know it's more likely that he doesn't care about hurting me, that maybe he's with another woman. Though it could have something to do with that takeover. Maybe he's in the middle of negotiations for work and simply forgot to tell me. That doesn't explain why his phone is off.

A metallic scraping sound comes from a door at the end of the row of chairs. The door whooshes opens, and in steps a tall, thin man—grey-haired, dressed in black trousers and a checkered business shirt, rolled up at the elbows.

He looks down at me. "You're the woman here about her husband?"

I nod before standing. "Marlys."

"I'm Officer Higgins. Come with me," he says sternly, and I follow him through the door to a large room filled with desks, to a back corner office.

Behind the desk, he sits in a swivel chair, leaning back and crossing an ankle over his other knee, and resting his interwoven fingers over his round abdomen. His eyes scan over me as I take the seat opposite him, cradling my bag as if it were a security blanket.

Our eyes meet, waiting, yet my mind races in circles, not knowing where to begin.

"I, uh..." I shake my head, tears prickling at the corners of my eyes.

"Start from the beginning," Officer Higgins says matter-of-factly, practically throwing a box of tissues in my direction.

Reaching for a tissue, I pull one free from the box and dab each eye before sucking in a deep breath. Our eyes meet again, and I rustle up as much courage as I can from every inch of my body.

"My husband went out Friday night, and he hasn't come home since. I've tried everything I can think of to find him, but... I don't know what more I can do. His phone's off now." My shoulders slump forward, eyes becoming wet again. "I'm worried something has happened to him."

With his thumb and forefinger, he rubs his chin. "Has he ever left like this before?"

"No, never," I say, hesitating. "He always lets me know if he's going to be late."

"Did he mention where he was going before he left?"

"He only went next door to speak to our neighbour about a work thing."

"Are you sure he's not still there, then?"

"Yes, I spoke with Xander already. He said Hunter—that's my husband—left his house in the early hours."

"Could he have come home and then left again before you woke up?"

I contemplate the suggestion for a second before replying. "I don't think so. His car was still at home."

"Perhaps he got a taxi or an Uber," he proposes.

Shrugging my shoulders, I really don't know. "He doesn't usually, but I suppose he could have."

"Right," Officer Higgins says, sitting upright in his chair, elbows resting on the desk, hands rubbing together. "Is there any chance he's involved in a work commitment? Perhaps it slipped your mind?"

My brows pull together as I try to think back to previous conversations I've had with Hunter this past week. I shake my head again. "No, I don't think so."

His forehead wrinkles, watching me closely. "Is there any chance he's involved with... someone else?"

Shuffling in my seat, I pull my bag closer to me, glancing away. "No... maybe... I don't know, honestly." Tears well again, then let loose, streaming down my face. He doesn't speak, just watches me, swiping the wetness away, but more tears come. Through the sobs, I find my way back to him, holding his gaze. "All I know is that my gut tells me something is wrong."

His head tilts slightly, then leans further over the desk. "Look, Marlys, I've been in this job a really long time, and I've seen just about every angle this type of situation can go."

I sniffle, wiping my nose with the now crumpled tissue. "And?"

He shakes his head. "From what little you've told me, my guess is that he'll be back in the next few days."

"What?" I say exasperated. "It's already been three days."

He nods. "Yes, I know. You mentioned that already. But hear me out. Your husband, Hunter, is it?"

"Yes, Hunter Brannigan."

Officer Higgins's face contorts, like hearing Hunter's name in full changes things all of a sudden.

"As in Brannigan Enterprises?" he asks curiously.

"Yes, that's his business. Why? Do you think that's connected to him going missing?"

He shakes his head dismissively. "Not at all. On the contrary. That just confirms my suggestion."

"What suggestion? You haven't said anything." My heart pounds against my chest, wishing he would just spit it out.

"Listen," he says, "I know you're worried about Mr Brannigan, and that you believe he's mixed up in something, but the reality is, CEOs of big businesses like his just don't 'go missing'." He says the last two words using air quotes, like I'm exaggerating now. Two minutes ago, I thought he was at least taking me seriously. Now? Dismissive. Patronising. Well, it's not good enough.

"But he has money. Lots of it. Someone could be blackmailing him, or—" I stutter, urgency fuelling my rushing words. "Or he could have been... *taken*. What if he's being held against his will."

"Stop," he says assertively, raising his voice, cutting me off. "Unless you've got some real evidence that indicates your husband is in actual trouble, then I suggest you go home and wait to hear from him."

I can't believe it. These people, the police, I thought they were meant to protect and serve. But from where I'm sitting, I can't see anything that looks like either of those. Appalling as it is, I'm clearly getting nowhere fast.

With clenched hands, I speak through gritted teeth. "Fine. If you won't help me, I'll find someone who will."

11

____

IN PURSUIT

MARLYS

My knuckles, now a pale shade, grip the steering wheel as if draining every ounce of life from it. The accelerator hovers close to the floor, pushing down, demanding the engine to roar louder. Swerving, I barely escape the pending collision with a delivery truck. The driver throws an arm out of the driver's side window, flipping me off. Under my breath, I curse the idiot.

Out of sight, my thoughts return to the police station. How stupid I was to think they'd be any use to me. So much for protecting and serving. From the looks of that guy, the only thing he's serving up is a big bunch of bullshit.

Skidding to a stop, I wait for the red light to turn green, fingers drumming against the steering wheel.

So, what do I do now?

Do I wait and see if Hunter comes home? Or find a private detective? I should've done that in the first place. But how was I to know the police would be useless to me?

Whatever I decide, I have to do it soon.

But where do I even begin?

Glancing down at the clock on the dashboard, I realise I'm going to be late picking up Kage from school. And on his first day back after being suspended.

Shit.

As if he doesn't hate me enough already. I'm practically handing him all the reasons to keep on it at this point.

Grabbing my phone from my bag on the passenger seat, I quickly scan the road and rear vision mirror, ensuring there's no police around, before tapping out a text to Kage. I drop the phone in the centre console, waiting for a reply.

I slow to take a left turn, when the phone vibrates. As the car straightens, I read his message: he's walking home.

It's not ideal, but I let him. With everything going on, arguing with my stepson isn't worth it. Refocussing on the road, I keep driving, but something nags at me, but I can't quite put my finger on it. I check the rear vision mirror before switching lanes. That's odd. I'm sure that black Escalade was behind me earlier, though SUVs are a dime a dozen in this town.

I brush it off, but they take the next turn, following me still. Is this the same SUV t I saw the other day? The one on our street. It had taken off too quickly for me to even get a glimpse at their number plate.

That was the day the note was left in our mailbox, addressed to Hunter. How on earth had I forgotten about that? It's strange that both the SUV and the note had turned up on the same day, and possibly within minutes of each other. Practically kicking myself, I should have given it to Hunter before the dinner party. Why didn't I? Would it make a difference now if I had?

Either way, I need to open it when I get home. Could its information lead me to my husband? But then again, what if it's something I don't want to know? I raise my hand, chewing at my nails before glancing again in the mirror. The SUV is still there.

It's undeniable now.

Hunter dragged me into a world where weird, bad, or just plain mysterious things are happening—and I have no clue what any of it means. Just two blocks from home, I need to think fast. My pulse races faster, gaze darting repeatedly between the road ahead and the SUV on my tail. Are they going to follow me all the way home? It'd be stupid to just lead them there, but if it's the same people, they already know our address. What do I do?

Trying to dodge them, I take the long way home, skirting the neighbourhood. Still, they follow. When I slow my car, they follow suit. When I accelerate, they do the same. I grab my phone and consider dialling the police—triple zero. But I see red, recalling their easy dismissal. They'd probably brush this off too, believing me paranoid. Maybe they'd drag me off for a psych evaluation. It's out of the question. I won't give them a second chance to make me look stupid.

Slowing to a crawl, I round the corner to our street, keeping the pace until I reach our driveway. I hesitate, giving way to another neighbour's car, before turning and pulling in. With the brake pulled on, I swivel in my seat to see the SUV drive past. Thank goodness for that. But what if they return?

I jump out, slam the Corolla's door, and sprint for the front door. I jab the Corolla's remote lock button as I run. My fingers fumble with my house keys, and I rush in the second it unlocks.

Heaving ragged breaths, I want to hide, yet my instincts tell me to stay. Prying a curtain aside, I peer out to the front yard, just as that same black SUV comes to a stop along the curb. My heart pounds in my chest, urging me to flee. Ordinarily I would, but with Hunter gone my life has been flipped on its head, and with that, I need to adapt.

What would Hunter do? Would he run? Hide?

No.

And since he's not here, someone has to protect us.

I need to do it myself.

Courage, it's what I need. To be brave. To find the strength to see the truth for what it is, to find the determination for answers, no matter how difficult they might be to accept.

Someone tall with a slim build exits the passenger seat, clad in a dark grey hoodie, pulled over their head, and matching sweatpants. I try to see their face, but they tilt their head forward, hiding it beneath the fabric. From the hoodie's front pocket, they retrieve something, looking around before placing it in my letterbox. Then retreat back to the SUV, but before they step in, their head turns to the side, staring directly at me for just a moment, then gets in the car, closing the door, hidden again by the windows' dark tint.

My hands tremble, legs like jelly, barely holding upright. What was that? A threat? Some sort of eerie acknowledgement?

I need to see what they left in the letterbox, but more importantly, I need to find Hunter's note from the other day. Where did I leave it? My mind is a scrambled mess, the past few days all blurring together. Where did I put it? On the bench? No, I didn't want to leave it where Kage could find it. Hunter's office? That's where I should've left it, but I never went in there that day. What was I doing? Come on Marlys, think.

Surely, I didn't leave it in my jeans pocket? No. But

then again, what else could I have done with it. Racing up the stairs to my bedroom, I dart into the ensuite, narrowing in on the dirty linen basket. Clothes fly about the space as I rip frantically through the pile until I reach the denim pants. Searching each pocket, one by one, my fingers finally tighten around folded paper in the back pocket. I pull it out, leaning against the vanity. It's the note.

I stare at the envelope in my hands, garnering the courage to open it. If Hunter comes home and sees I've opened his mail, there'll be hell to pay, but if it holds a clue to his whereabouts, then isn't it worth it? I truly don't know the answer, or want to find out. Yet the longer I look at it, the more urgent it feels. I have to see what's inside. Maybe I can read it without opening it? I switch on the light and hold the envelope up to it, but it's useless.

Sighing with defeat, I turn it over to the back, and slip a finger under the flap, slowing tearing it open. My stomach churns with nervous energy, fingers twitching as they lock onto the note inside, pulling it free from its prison. Unfolding it—the same elegant cursive stares back at me.

Tell us where she is. One way or the other you will.

12

THE SECOND WARNING
MARLYS

"What does it say?" Xander asks from the other end of his couch. With his ankle crossed over one knee, he leans back against the cushions.

Hunched over with elbows on my knees, I stare at the note between my fingers. "I already showed you."

"No, the other one."

I shake my head. "I haven't opened it yet."

He furrows his brow, rubbing his chin. "What's stopping you?"

My shoulders slump as I let out a deep sigh. "Honestly, I'm scared."

"Hmm, I suppose I'd be concerned too, if I were you. But aren't you the least bit curious?"

"Well, yeah. Of course. I just... I don't know. It all feels a bit... too much. You know?"

Tilting his head, he narrows his focus on me. "Do you want me to do the honours?"

"Would you? If you don't mind."

Xander shuffles along the couch, hand out, ready to take

the note. Yet something prevents me from passing it to him, like it's glued to my fingertips.

"Well?" he says, still holding his palm out to me.

"Sorry, here." Rubbing my hands together in a ball, I inch closer to the couch's edge, watching him pry the envelope open.

His gaze flicks up at me, like he's checking I'm alright before continuing. He frees the note, unfolding it carefully. Watching his eyes scan across the page, nervous energy urges one leg to bounce erratically. Xanders brow furrows and his jaw clenches.

"What is it?" I ask, almost whispering. The longer he waits to fill me in on the contents of the note, the more worried I become. My pulse races feverishly as my mind jumps to conclusions.

At long last, his gaze flicks up over the note. "Do you want me to read it to you, or..."

I nod. "Please."

He clears his throat and sits up straighter. "This is your last warning. Tell us where she is, or we'll destroy everything you love."

There's that word again—'she'. I have no clue who it's referring to. But one thing is for certain. Hunter does. I wish there was some clue in the note to tell me who 'she' is, or what her relationship is to Hunter. Without him here—will I ever know?

A picture of Kage appears in my mind. He could be in harm's way, too. That's assuming they meant us. What sort of monster threatens a child? Either way, I have to do something to ensure our safety. But what?

"What do you make of that, then?" Xander asks.

"I don't know. Who are they even talking about?" I shake my head in frustration.

"Hunter must've known," he says like he's thinking out loud rather than to me.

"Why didn't he tell me he or we were being threatened?" The truth hisses in my ear.. Hunter kept his secrets close. So close, that even I didn't know of their existence. For six months, we'd been slipping further apart, trust unravelling thread by thread like a rope fraying under too much strain. Or had he never trusted me at all?

Xander shuffles along the couch to my side. Wrapping an arm around my shoulders—a friendly gesture—I let myself lean into him. His knee rubs against mine as quiet tears fall. He pulls me in tighter, shushing me tenderly. Wiping my nose with a tissue crumpled up from inside my bra, my hand falls along with a deep sigh. Still clutching the tissue, my hand rests on his thigh, unknowingly. It's only when his other hand, warm and comforting, engulfs mine, that I'm even aware of the added touch. This is new. Different, and precariously dangerous. I like it too much. I shouldn't. Not with everything that's going on.

Temptation, and lust—they're the devils own, aren't they? Alluring in far too many ways.

I can't. I shouldn't.

Retrieving my hand, I sit up straighter, turning slightly to look up at him. Watching him for a response. To see if it's all in my head, or if he's really making a move.

"You okay?" he asks, brushing a stray hair from my eyes.

My gaze darts back and forth, trying to read him. It's futile, and I force a small smile as I nod. "Yeah, I just... What if this isn't over? What if whomever wrote these notes thinks I know something?"

Xander leans back, withdrawing his arm. "Do you?"

"No, of course not. I had no idea about any of this. But now... I have no choice but to deal with it."

"You're stronger than you know, Marlys. But I'm here, for whatever it is that you need."

"Thanks. I need to speak to Kage. Let him know what's going on."

Xander tilts his head, rubbing his chin for a moment, brows furrowing like he's considering something. "You should stay here tonight. You and Kage."

"Uh, I don't know..."

"Or I could take the couch at yours. To put your mind at ease. But it's completely up to you."

I shake my head. "I can't ask you to do that."

"You didn't. I offered."

"Okay, then. Just for tonight, if you're sure?" My gaze wanders to Xander's lounge room window. My heart hammers in my chest, fixated on the space. "Xander," I whisper, "Look."

He follows my line of sight until he reaches the window, but it's gone as fast as I saw it.

"What was it?" he asks.

"I think I saw someone."

Xander jumps to his feet, moving towards the door. He peeks through the window, scanning the street without a word. Then he turns, facing me, with a solemn expression. "Lock the doors."

13

____

CURIOUS THINGS

MARLYS

Before his disappearance, we'd been safe with Hunter. Despite all the times I'd felt alone, miserable, lost in this house, he'd been there. Even when engrossed in business in his office, he was always there, on the other side of the door. Just like Kage, hidden in his room, his presence gave an ounce of comfort. That I wasn't alone. Even with the downsides, he was there. My husband, my once true love.

Oh, how my heart aches for him now.

Not just for the Hunter I first met. The one who love-bombed me into his world, his embrace. But for the one he is now.

Holding back the grief of his absence, retaining the calm demeanour for Kage. It's demanding, infuriating, but most of all, it's just plain exhausting.

Maybe when he returns, when I find him again, we can go back to that. To the beginning.

But for now, all I can do is keep moving.

Standing alongside Xander at his front window, we wait until he's satisfied it's safe to head home.

Kage arrives, walking down the footpath as we leave Xander's place. My pulse races, scanning the street, but there's nothing out of the ordinary. No SUV this time. But there's nothing urgent about Kage's pace, strolling up the walkway to the house, bag hanging over one shoulder.

Inside, I reach for the lock, but Xander's already ahead of me. He takes one last glance through the window before following me into the house.

"Kage, honey," I say, hand resting on the balustrade, interrupting him, already halfway up the stairs. He pauses, looking over his shoulder, unimpressed. "Will you have dinner down here tonight, please? I need to discuss something with you." His brow rises. I know that look. He's not interested, planning to lock himself away in his room as usual. I sigh. "Please, it's important."

"Fine," he huffs. "Text me when it's ready."

I force a smile even though I'm falling apart inside, then head into the kitchen.

Xander stands at the end of the table, leaning against it, arms crossed. "Why do you let him walk all over you like that?"

I pull items from the refrigerator for dinner. "I don't."

"Hmm," he says, with a disagreeable tone.

I grab a peeler from the drawer and begin slicing off the carrot's rough skin. "What's that supposed to mean?" I'm defensive, and I can't bring myself to make eye contact.

He sucks in a deep breath, letting it out through his nose. "Have you thought about what you're going to tell Kage?"

Resting my hands on the bench top, I look up at him. "No, not really." I pick up a potato and start peeling that. "I'll have to tell him about Hunter, but..." I sigh. "I'm not sure how much to tell him about the other stuff."

The kitchen is quiet, except for the sounds of dinner prep, for a long minute. My mind filters through my options, to no avail. "Do you have any advice?"

Xander moves from standing and drags a chair out from the table. He sits, staring at the ceiling, considering his guidance. "He's sixteen. I think your best bet is to tell him the truth."

"How much truth, though?"

"All of it."

"All of it? The note? The threat? The SUV?" I ask, incredulous. My grip tightens around the peeler. He nods. I shake my head.

"You asked for my advice, that's it. But do whatever you think is best."

Pulling out two stainless steel pots, and another pan, I place them on the stovetop, turning the knobs. With the pot filler, I fill the one for the potatoes. "The thing is, if I tell him everything, will he take it seriously? Or will he just brush it off like it doesn't concern him? I mean, yes, he's sixteen. Old enough to understand the danger, but he's also young enough to think he's untouchable. You know how kids are. I don't want to scare him. But I need him to be careful. Honestly, Xander, where's the line between protection and paranoia?"

"At the end of the day, all you can do is tell him the truth and hope he listens."

Half an hour later, I send a quick text to Kage letting him know dinner is ready.

At the table, Kage takes his usual seat facing the window. I sit opposite, with Xander beside me.

"Thanks for cooking, Marlys. It's so nice to have a home-cooked meal for a change. Well, one I didn't have to cook myself," Xander remarks.

"You're welcome," I say, then turn to Kage, who's poking around the plate with his fork. "Is there something wrong with your meal?"

"It's fine," he says, not meeting my gaze. Scooping a mouthful of mashed potato, he finally looks up, glancing at me and Xander. "I thought you wanted to talk about something?" He shovels the food in his mouth.

It's the most attention he's paid me in months, and I shift uncomfortably in my seat. "Uh, yeah. We wanted to talk about..."

"Dad?" he says, cutting me off. "I know." He takes another mouthful and chews.

"You know?"

"Yeah."

"What do you mean?"

Kage puts his fork down, clinking against the plate, and swallows his mouthful. His brows pull together. "Come on, Marlys. You can't be that stupid, surely?"

"Kage," Xander says in a low voice, as if telling him to watch his mouth.

Rolling his eyes, Kage goes on. "All I'm saying is that people talk. Kids at school, people around town. It's not a secret."

"What did you hear?"

His eyes scan me as if he's trying to figure out what exactly I know, whether his next words will be new and frightening, or whether I know too. He looks away. "Just that he ran off with his girlfriend, or something like that."

"Really?" I ask, maintaining my composure. But inside I'm screaming. My pulse rises, grip tightening around my fork. How the hell does he even know this?

"Not exactly surprising, is it?" Kage stabs at his food. "He's an asshole."

My eyes widen, shocked at the revelation. Our family is the town gossip, but more shocking is the fact he knew about this and never told me. It shouldn't surprise me though. It's not like we've ever been close before.

"There's more to it than that," I say. "And I need you to be on high alert."

Kage shakes his head. "That's ridiculous. What do you think is going to happen? That he's going to come back and kidnap me." He laughs. "As if."

"It's not that." I suck in a deep breath, steadying myself. "Your dad, well, he's been getting strange notes. The last one was threatening."

His brows furrow. "What kind of notes? Like from his girlfriend, or like a stalker?"

"I'm not sure, more like the latter, I suppose. But until I know more—until I figure out what's going on here—I need you to be safe."

"I walked home today, and I was fine."

Xander interjects. "There's also been someone following Marlys. A black SUV. She saw it parked out the front of here a couple of times now as well."

I frown at Xander, giving out information I wasn't even sure I wanted to tell. Then glance back at Kage. "I don't know who they are, or what they want, other than what's in the note."

"What's it say then? Can I see it?" Kage asks.

"There's no reason for that. But if you must know, it refers to a woman."

"And?" Kage asks.

I sigh. "Whomever they are, think your dad knows where 'she' is." My fingers curl up like quotation marks.

"What the fuck?" Kage says.

"Kage," Xander scolds again.

He rolls his eyes at Xander. "What do you mean knows where 'she' is? Do they think dad kidnapped a woman?"

"I really don't know what they think. Just that he knows where she is, and he won't tell them. And because of that... secret, I guess, they're threatening our family."

"Don't you think you should go to police?"

"I went to the police already about your dad. They weren't interested in helping us find him." A tear wells in my eye, and I dab at it with my finger.

"Did you tell them about the note? The car you saw?"

"Well, no." I press my fingers to my temples, trying to think. "I was upset, Kage. I went in there hoping they'd help, and when they didn't, I just–I don't know, it slipped my mind."

Kage laughs. "Bullshit, Marlys." He narrows his eyes. "You know more than you're letting on."

I stiffen, gripping the edge of the table. "What? No. I don't. Everything I've told you is what I know."

Kage exhales through his nose, shaking his head. "Why do you even care? He was a dick to you. To me. To everyone. Whatever. You're probably happy he's gone. I am."

Xander's chair scrapes against the floor as he shifts. "That's enough, Kage." His voice is firm, leaving no room for argument.

Kage scoffs and pushes back from the table. "Whatever. Believe what you want." He heads over to the stairs, leaving without another word.

Exhaling the breath I'd been holding, I try to rid myself of the mounting tension. But it's still there, like a heavy weight, pressing down on me. Suffocating me.

"He's hiding something," I mutter.

"Or he just doesn't care," Xander retorts.

But I don't think that's the case at all. Maybe he's just hurting. He was abandoned by his mother, and now it's as if his father has done the same. My heart aches for him, but I don't know how to ease his burden.

A soft thump sound comes from Hunter's home office, on the other side of the room.

I freeze, staring at the door. Xander turns instinctively towards the noise, watching for a moment. He turns back to me, as if he's confirming I heard it too.

"Tell me that was just Liquorice," I whisper, but dread coils in my stomach.

At the mention of her name, the cats head appears, popping up from the vacant chair opposite Xander. Her mouth opens wide as she yawns, then pounces onto the tabletop with a tiny meow.

"Doesn't seem like it," Xander says sarcastically.

My stomach knots, and I swallow hard, forcing myself to breath despite the growing heaviness in the air. Xanders arm rests on the table, and I grab it. If I say it out loud, he's going to think I'm ridiculous–crazy even. But I've put up with second guessing myself over this for the past year. I can't ignore it anymore. "Xander," I say, trying to summon the courage to say it. "I think this house is haunted."

My hand trembles. Xander places his other hand on top to.

"Come on, Marlys. Haunted?" He shakes his head.

"I'm serious."

He tilts his head. "You actually believe that?"

"Ever since I moved in here, I've heard noises, and I get creepy feelings in different rooms, and sometimes things move on their own. It's not just my imagination, Xander. I think it's... Amelia."

"What makes you think it's Amelia?" His brows furrow.

I hesitate for a second before answering, starting to feel foolish for telling him. "Who else would it be?"

"Marlys, Amelia isn't..." He stops, exhales, shaking his head. "Look, I don't know what Hunter told you about her, but..." He looks up, meeting my gaze. "Last time I saw her, she was alive."

My breath catches in my throat then I force out the word. "What?"

My stomach sinks.

Another thump. Louder this time.

My pulse rises, mind racing. Xander's breath hitches beside me.

"Still think it's a ghost?" he murmurs under his breath.

I don't know what to believe anymore. If I was wrong about Amelia, what else have I been wrong about?

14

INBOX OF LIES

MARLYS

I hate the way my ears ring when the silence is too much. If it wasn't for the mumble of voices from the TV, as the credits roll on, it would be just like that. Every minuscule sound jars me from relaxation, from sleep. I should head upstairs, to the comfort of my own bed but the thought of Hunter's prolonged absence from it sends a chill up my spine.

Xander's still here, 'protecting' us from the unknown terrors outside. Yet we're still no closer to finding Hunter.

I sit up from where I'd been resting during the movie. His arm remains curled around the pillow where my head rested. Grabbing the small throw I'd been using, I drape it over him but it's too small to cover his legs. It doesn't reach his shoulders either.

I have to thank my lucky stars for him. He's such a good friend. I'm sure he'd give the shirt off his back to anyone who needs it, but for me, well, I know he'd go the extra mile. Not that I would expect him to. No, I'd never ask that of him.

My cheeks warm, watching him. He doesn't stir.

Something in my chest follows suit. When no one else is around, I can allow myself to feel it. But not for too long. That wouldn't be right.

Looking around the room, my gaze wanders to the ceiling, to upstairs. Kage didn't comeback down after dinner, not for dessert, and not for the movie. He's safe though, with Xander down here guarding our home, with me.

I move quietly towards the kitchen. I'm sure there's still some camomile tea tucked away in the back of the pantry. Hopefully, sleep will come if I have a cup.

My mind shifts back to Hunter and a cold tendril of anxiety curls in my stomach. These past few days—or is has it been a week? I don't rightly remember now—but it's been challenging. No matter how much I pretend like I've got it all together, the not knowing is eating at me.

I sit at the kitchen island, sipping the tea until it's done. I should go to bed, but in all honesty, I want to be close to Xander tonight. To keep me safe, if only in appearance.

Returning to the lounge, I snuggle back in beside him. His arm pulls me in closer as I settle, closing my eyes.

Just for a minute. A hand brushes against my cheek.

I shouldn't allow him to touch me like that, so I feign sleep despite the touch snapping me wide awake. But there's no encore.

Opening my eyes just a sliver, I tip my head to the side. He's still asleep, TV still on but muted. Xander hasn't moved an inch.

I can't make sense of it—perhaps it was my imagination. Just a dream. But then I recall fragmented pieces from my slumber.

Hunter.

He'd been in my dream. But the more I try to recall the

details, the faster they seem to slip away. The hair on my skin prickles. Something isn't right.

I glance up at the clock above the TV—it's 3 am, precisely.

Focused on my breathing. I can't keep waking up like this in the middle of the night. How many restless nights have I had? Three or four? I've lost count.

This is beyond a joke now. I need answers. Something concrete.

Perhaps Hunter's home office holds a clue.

I sit up, squinting through the darkened area by the kitchen where his office is, daring myself to look. No one else will do this for me. I need to be bold, strong. Figure this out for myself.

Slipping off the couch, careful not to disturb Xander, I head to the office door. My fingers hesitate on the handle.

Hunter would lose his mind if he knew I was going in here. Messing with his stuff. Even after we were married, this was his private space. And I let him have it. I suppose it was his way of having independence in the marriage, even as mine blurred until I wasn't sure where I fit anymore.

I shake off the thought and push the door open.

Inside, the air is stale. Despite the few days since its use, the room feels eerie and abandoned. The desk chair is slightly turned where Hunter had last sat. Laptop still squarely centred on top, surrounded by papers and files.

Shifting towards the desk, I look around, trying to figure out where to start. What am I even looking for?

Starting with a stack of files on the left side of the desk, I flip through contracts, financial records, and meeting minutes. None of it means anything to me. Beside it sits a stack of mail. A few envelopes have been torn open, while others sit untouched. Sifting through them, nothing strikes me as odd

A cold shiver runs down my back and a strange feeling of being watched hovers over me. My heart hammers in my chest. Over my shoulder, I check the doorway.

Kage stands there, arms crossed, brows furrowed. "Geez, Marlys. What the hell are you doing in here?"

"I'm looking for answers. Trying to figure out what happened to your dad."

He shakes his head. "You're wasting your time."

"You don't know that," I snap back.

"He's gone. You really think digging through his paperwork is going to change that?"

"Maybe," I say, almost whispering. My eyes sting, but I force the tears back.

Kage takes a step closer. "He's probably lying on a beach somewhere, living his best life without us."

"I refuse to believe that, Kage. There has to be more to it. Something's wrong, I know it."

"And what if the truth is that he's just an asshole, and he abandoned us? What then?"

I don't know how to answer that. I've been holding onto the hope that there's some reason he's not here, that something or someone is preventing his return. But Kage has a point. What if he hasn't returned because he simply doesn't want to? Doesn't want either of us in his life anymore?

Burying my head in my hands, desperately trying to stop the wave of tears teetering on the edge of flowing. But it's no use. A stream flows down my cheeks. With the back of my hand, I wipe them away, sniffling.

Kage huffs and steps closer. "Move over," he says, sounding thoroughly defeated.. "You won't find shit in that pile of papers. If you want answers, you need to get into his laptop."

He drops into the chair, switching the laptop on. Behind him, I stand, watching him tap away the first attempt at the password. It's not right. Kage tries again, but that one's wrong too. A warning tells us we'll be locked out if our third attempt fails. But Kage tries anyway. This time, we're in.

A variety of applications flash as the computer starts up, Kage dismissing each one to the bottom bar.

"What are you doing?" I ask, worried he's going to miss something important.

He clicks on a blue icon. "We don't need that crap, start with his email."

The screen loads: folders appear on the left third, and the contents of each email fill the remaining space. Kage shifts closer to the screen. His throat rumbles as he considers what he's looking at.

"What is it?" I ask with urgency.

"There's two email accounts here. This one is his work email," he says, pointing at the screen where it reads CEO@branniganenterprises.com then he clicks on the screen. "And this one looks personal." It simply reads hunterb123@gmail.com. "Which one do you want to look at first?"

I consider for a moment. "Let's try his work one. Something was off during the dinner party before he... left."

"Right," Kage mumbles. "The one I wasn't allowed to go to. I remember."

I place a hand on his shoulder apologetically. And for once, he doesn't shrug me away.

The email inbox is filled with hundreds of unread messages. Business updates, meeting confirmations, forwarded documents from his assistant. None of which is unusual. I notice a few from Brielle regarding the sale of her and Grayson's business, but that's about it.

"Let's try the other email," I suggest to Kage.

He clicks a few times and Hunter's personal email inbox loads. Scrolling down, every second email appears to be some sort of spam, alternating with receipts from online purchases, and subscription services, dotted with updates from others. But then Kage clicks on one from a care home an hour away.

"What's that about?" I ask.

Kage moves down the page, reading the cover email. It's generic and simply asks for a prompt payment of the overdue balance, referring to an attached PDF document.

The mouse hovers over the PDF. "Open it?" he asks.

"Go ahead," I reply.

The itemised lines include service fees and dates referring to monthly periods. Additional charges appear at the bottom: pharmacy and medication costs, GP consultations, and smaller expenses like TV subscriptions and craft supplies. Below that is the total amount owing. My breath catches in my throat as I read the five-figure sum. "Oh, my God."

"Wow, that's some serious money," Kage remarks, clearly surprised too. "But I don't understand what it is." He spins the chair to face me. "Do you know?"

"It looks like he's been paying for someone in a care home. Did you see a name on there?"

"Nope, nothing that stands out."

"Can you go back to the top? Go slower this time. I want to make sure we didn't miss anything."

"Sure." Kage does as I ask, and I scour each word of the document. "Could it be for my grandma?"

"No, I don't think so. I'm pretty sure your dad said she's in a local care home." I pause for a moment, realising this might be the first time he's ever mentioned his grandmother to me. "Kage, do you recall ever meeting her?"

"No, but I've seen pictures of her holding me when I was little."

"Oh," I say, not knowing what else to say to that.

Kage scrolls through the document. "Here." He points at the reference on the invoice. "It says A. Brannigan."

My breath catches in my throat, stomach reeling.

Amelia.

That name. That impossible name.

The hairs on the back of my neck prickled as the room grows cooler.

"No," I whisper.

"What?" Kage asks curiously.

I scan the name again and again. It's not possible. She's dead. Amelia is dead. She has to be. I convinced myself of it for the longest time. The strange noises in the house—creaking, whispers and breaths. That ominous feeling of someone always watching. I thought it was her. A ghost.

But ghosts have no use for money.

"Marlys? Who the hell is Amelia?"

My gaze doesn't falter as I stare at him. He should know who she is, and her name. She was his mother, after all.

I thought Hunter told me something terrible had happened to her.

And maybe it had.

But not in the way I thought.

"This doesn't make sense."

Kage's brows pulled together. "What doesn't?"

I swallowed hard, trying to piece it together. If Amelia

was alive, why had Hunter never mentioned her? Why did I believe she was dead and haunting me?

Unless... someone had wanted me to believe that.

Hunter lied.

My stomach knots, uneasy.

Xander said Amelia was alive when he last saw her. But how'd that happen if she's in a care home? Surely Hunter hadn't let him visit. Had he gone looking for her?

Perhaps Xander's been lying to me, too.

He wouldn't, would he?

"We need more than this," I say.

"More than what?"

"The invoice doesn't tell us anything except that she's alive. We need to see the records. We need to know *why* she's there."

And, most importantly, I need to know why Hunter let me believe she was dead.

Because if he hid this from me, what else had he been hiding?

15

THE MORE YOU KNOW...
MIRANDA

Marlys has no clue that I'm here. Following her. She never does.

Today is different. More important than those that came before. One I can't miss.

She moves slowly through the care home, like she's tiptoeing through crocodiles, careful not to get bitten. Her grip is tight around her purse strings, bracing herself.

I don't need to follow her. At least, not in the way she thinks.

I meet her there.

Slipping between the spaces, to exist in the periphery is easy. I spent a lot of time learning how. Shifting in the places no one thinks to look, and lingering in the cracks of their uncertainty.

That's how I watch her now.

She doesn't notice the shifting temperature as I pass through the entrance. She doesn't shudder the way I've seen her do before.

Marlys approaches the reception area in the foyer. I

hold back, allowing the distance between us to grow. She fumbles with her purse strap, searching for words.

"Hi," she says with a strained smile to the woman behind the desk.

"How can I help you?" the woman asks.

"I, uh, my husband received an overdue invoice, and..."

"You'll need to see the facility manager about financial queries," she announces, her voice matter-of-fact, like a recorded version she's said a thousand times before.

Marlys falters, brushing her hair behind her ear. "Actually, I was hoping to visit someone."

The woman's brows rise high on her forehead. "Are you on the approved visitor list?"

"There's a list?"

She nods, then narrows her eyes, scrutinising her. "We must vet and approve all visitors to ensure our clients' privacy."

Marlys scans the room like she's searching for answers, then wipes her palms against her thighs. It's almost laughable. I can't believe she came here without a plan. But I've seen her bullshit her way out of trouble before—with Hunter—maybe she'll have some of that magic today as well.

She leans over the counter and lowers her voice. I shift a little closer. Just enough to hear her.

"My husband, Hunter, well, he's not available right now. I need to speak with... Amelia."

"Amelia?" the woman asks.

"Yes, Amelia Brannigan."

"Really?" she asks, like she doesn't believe Marlys.

Nodding, Marlys continues. "Yes, she's the mother of my stepson."

"And your name?" the woman asks, tapping on the keyboard in front of her.

"Marlys Brannigan."

The woman scans the screen, then taps some more, moving the mouse around, before returning her attention to Marlys.

"There's no mention of you on the visitor list. And," her head tips forward. "There's no mention of any children."

She considers the woman's words for a minute. "I imagine Hunter forgot to update it after the wedding. I really need to see her. I'll be quick, I promise."

The woman frowns. "I'll take you to see her this one time, but if she doesn't want to see you, then you must leave—immediately. Understood?"

"Yes, absolutely. Thank you so much."

The woman marches down the corridor. Marlys races to keep up. They push through two large double doors to another area where a large sign displays the ward's name—*Harmony East*.

"Her room is just down here," the woman says, ushering Marlys along.

Rooms line the corridor; some doors closed, others are ajar or wide open. All with names of their resident client. Finally, they reach a door that reads '*Amelia B*'.

"Here we are," the woman says. "Wait here while I speak with Amelia."

Marlys nods, her hands clasped in front of her, standing at attention like a schoolgirl waiting outside the principal's office.

A few moments later, she reappears, and guides Marlys inside.

"This is Marlys," she says to Amelia, then turns to face Marlys. "Amelia is a little tired today. Please keep it brief."

The woman leaves Marlys standing in the centre of the room, while Amelia rests in a wheelchair by a window overlooking the gardens. A small, crocheted throw covers her legs, and hands rest on the armrest. She's aged since I last came here. Silver streaks run through her once long blonde hair, now trimmed at the jawline. Though when she turns her head to face Marlys, a thinner patch is visible. There's just enough hair covering it to obscure the scar that I know marks her body. Forever a reminder of that night.

I'm not sure Marlys has noticed it. It's doubtful since she doesn't know what I do. Has seen what I have, what Amelia has.

The dark circles around her eyes are new, but she's fared well enough with no wrinkles. Though the small smile she gives Marlys travels to her eyes where thin lines crease.

"Do I know you?" she asks. Her voice is the same—melodic and smooth. Yet, the pacing seems off, slower.

Marlys's head tilts, taking in Amelia's appearance. Her eyes dart towards the door, then back again. Then her brows furrow, and her head shakes ever so slightly.

I wish I could read her mind right now. To see what's going on in that head of hers. Not to mention how rude she's being, ignoring Amelia's question.

"Hello?" Amelia says, snapping Marlys back to reality.

Clutching a hand to her chest, Marlys gasps. "Oh, my goodness, I'm so sorry. It's just, well, you're different from how I imagined you." Her cheeks flushing pink as she stretches a hand out in greeting. "I'm Marlys. It's lovely to meet you."

She takes her hand, loosely shaking it before letting go. "Please sit," Amelia says, waving towards a chair. "Thank you for coming to see me. It's been so long since I've had a visitor. But you'll have to forgive me. I'm not sure how we know each other."

Marlys shuffles in the seat, crossing her legs at the ankles. "Well, actually, we haven't officially met." She pauses for a second, like she's watching Amelia closely for a reaction, before continuing. "I'm Hunter's wife."

Amelia remains graceful and unmoving, almost. Except for the slight shift on her forehead, the shadow of a frown. Her gaze shifts towards the doorway, towards me. Like she sees me, not through me. Panic coils through me. But then she returns to Marlys.

"For a moment, I thought you were someone else. You look so much like her," Amelia says.

"Who did you think I was?" Marlys asks.

Amelia bides her time, then a soft smile curls. "Have you seen her?"

Marlys frowns, as if she's thrown off by the question. "Seen who?"

"The one who came before me," Amelia says softly, then lets out a long sigh. "Miranda."

Marlys stills and lips part, but no words come out. Brows knitting together tighter as she shakes her head.

She doesn't know the name, or the person. She doesn't know me. And until this moment, my existence was nothing but an occasional eerie feeling.

The insult stabs at my core. A forgotten remnant. It's enough to fuel my ire, the tiny flicker igniting, daring to grow into a raging fire. To burn it all down. To the ground.

"I don't know who that is," Marlys says in a low voice. But I hear her loud and clear.

"Then you haven't been paying attention."

With one hand, Marlys rubs goose pimples on her forearms. "I'm sorry. What are you talking about?"

"She haunts you, doesn't she?" Amelia's words sound like a question, but it's rhetorical.

Marlys stiffens and sits up straighter in the chair. "What?"

An empathetic smile lights up Amelia's face, and her words are warm and pitying. "I was haunted too." Her gaze drifts up to the ceiling like she's remembering in vivid detail. "Strange noises, feeling like I was being watched, and cold spots—like the one you just felt."

Her eyes widen, mouth agape, hanging onto every syllable as Amelia speaks. Her hands drift to her thighs, fingers curling as she bows her head, contemplating. She breathes deep—in and out—in and out—until she steadies herself. Then she lifts her gaze, locking eyes with Amelia.

"You're probably thinking my traumatic brain injury has gotten the best of me. That I've imagined it all," Amelia says. "I thought that too... at first. But it couldn't be. I was experiencing all that before... my injury."

"Amelia," Marlys whispers, then sighs. "I'm so sorry. I shouldn't have come here stirring up the past." She shakes her head. "I'm sorry for everything you've been through. But ghosts?" A small laugh escapes her. "Please get some rest. I'll get out of your hair." Marlys stands, straightening her shirt, before taking a step towards the door.

"Marlys," Amelia says. She turns to face her. "You should leave."

"Leave? Why?"

"Before something terrible happens to you, too."

I stay in the doorway as Marlys walks away. Amelia watches too, but her focus isn't on her.

It's on me.

She stares—not through me. At me. And I *don't* like it.

I need to get out of here.

Keeping my distance, I return to the foyer. Observing from the periphery.

Marlys' hands ball by her sides, head turned down as she passes through. Though she raises her head slightly towards reception. The woman who'd quizzed her earlier, is doing the same with a man. He's tall, wearing a dark-coloured track suit, hoodie covering his head. Like Marlys, his hands are balled into fists, propped aggressively on the desk top, but the woman maintains a calm demeanour. This is obviously not her first time dealing with difficult visitors.

"I need to see my sister," he says, growling out the words.

"As I told you before, only approved visitors..."

He cuts her off, voice growing louder and more urgent. "I don't give a damn about your list. I'm family."

She places a hand between his, asserting her control, but her face remains composed. "I understand, but you need approval..."

Again he speaks over the top of her. Her jaw clenches as he bangs on the bench. "I don't need approval to see my own bloody sister."

Marlys flinches at the bang, yet she stands observing the interaction.

The woman let's out a frustrated breath. "Look, just speak with her power of attorney, and get them to approve you."

He bangs the bench-top again, turning to leave. Storming through the foyer, he shoves past an information stand, knocking it over, sending flyers skittering across the tiled floor. He flings open the front double doors; they crash against the guardrail and swing shut with a metallic clang.

Marlys pulls the strap of her bag higher over her

shoulder, then heads towards the exit. Once through the door, she stops again, staring off to the right.

About fifty metres away is the man. In one hand he has a mobile phone to his ear, the other holding a cigarette. He puffs as he speaks, pacing back and forth. Only bits and pieces of the conversation are audible, but his tone is clear—he's fuming.

Picking up her pace, Marlys almost runs to her car, only stopping to unlock the car door. But she chances a look back.

His gaze snaps to her. Direct and unflinching. Measured. Like he's deciding whether to close the distance between them.

She must notice it, too. Hiking herself into the driver's seat, Marlys hurries to lock each door. The engine roars to life. What will he do next?

He steps forward. Then takes two more steps.

His steps continue. Pace quickening with each move.

Until he's jogging, then running.

Marlys' hands tremble, struggling to shift the car into gear, her knuckles turn white gripping the steering wheel.

There's almost no distance between them now.

Marlys stomps hard on the accelerator, ripping the car from its park, roaring over the gravelled lot, and onto the road.

He curses, but she doesn't hear it—but I do.

He turns, heading for his SUV.

Black paint, tinted windows, a familiar sticker on the rear windshield.

I know that SUV, and so does Marlys.

She thinks she's escaping, but my gut tells me this is far from over.

16

THE WEIGHT OF SPECULATION

KAGE

I can't remember the last time Dad and Marlys were both absent from our house. For once I can do whatever I like without worrying about him saying some passive aggressive bullshit or how much of a shit son I am. And Marlys, with her ever present hovering, like she's some sort of mother figure, or whatever.

Nope, today I can actually watch something on the huge seventy-five-inch TV, lounging around on the couch, rather than laying on my bed watching Netflix on my ten-inch computer screen. To top it off, I found a party sized bag of Twisties hidden in the pantry. Shovelling chips into my mouth, I'm glued to the screen at the midpoint of the latest superhero movie. Sound effects boom through the surround sound speakers, and for once I'm happy they went all out on expensive shit.

Marlys races into the room. I hadn't heard her get home or unlock the door. Oddly, she doesn't acknowledge me or say 'Hi'. She just heads straight to the coffee table, grabbing the remote and changing the channel.

"What the hell, Marlys? I was watching that."

She doesn't answer. Focussed on the screen, she flips through the channels, like she's searching for something. Finally, she stops.

A local broadcaster is airing a 'breaking news' live feed.

"Hey," I yell, trying to get her attention.

"Shh," she asserts without pulling her eyes away from the screen.

I turn towards the screen, still furious at the interruption. Along the bottom of the screen runs a ribbon of text:

'Chilling discovery: Body found in shallow grave'.

Too many questions race through my mind. How'd she even know about this? Didn't she go to that care home about the invoice? Or was she up to something else entirely?

My gaze returns to Marlys, and I narrow my eyes, gauging her reaction. The remote trembles in her hands like she's close to this somehow.

The reporter's voice directs me back to the screen where a woman is centred, microphone in hand. A flurry of police officers and vehicles behind her. She clears her throat and speaks in a calm, professional manner.

"Authorities were called to this location earlier today after a member of the public discovered what appears to be a shallow grave. While police have not yet released an official statement, sources indicate that a body has been recovered at the site. Given the proximity to town and the timeline of its discovery, speculation has already begun regarding whether this could be linked to missing CEO and businessman Hunter Brannigan..."

Dad? My brain freezes. The reporter's lips move but I don't comprehend the words.

Dad? They think... Dad? All the air in my lung's escapes, pain reeling through me. As much as I hate him, as much as I wanted him gone, this is next level. I don't know what to think about this. Or how to feel.

Marlys lets out a strangled voice. "Oh, my God." Her knees buckle beneath her, and she falls into a heap in the middle of the lounge room floor. Her hands covering her face, hair flying everywhere as she breaks down like I've never seen before.

I should be breaking down like this, too.

A small piece of me thinks she's overreacting. That she should feel relieved—free. But another part of me sickens with guilt for even thinking that. I'm not sure how she's going to get through this. Or even if I can.

I should say something. Do something.

A picture of my dad smiling and shaking hands with some other business guy floods the TV screen. He looks alive, not buried in some shallow grave.

Not... My thoughts trail off, and my chest tightens.

They don't know for sure that it's him. They even said 'speculation'.

They haven't even identified the body yet. There's nothing to get worked up about.

But everybody's thinking it. Whispering it. Feeding off our pain like vultures.

Looking back at Marlys, crumpled on the floor, I know I should say something. Tell her it's too soon to assume, that people always jump to conclusions. I try to find the words to comfort her, but before I can stop myself, the thought spews out.

"Took them long enough."

Marlys turns to me, wide eyed and blotchy. "What did you just say?"

Ordinarily, I wouldn't give a shit what she thinks. But today is not an ordinary day. I've fucked up. I know it; she knows it. There's no recovering from this. My stomach knots, churns. The Twisties swirl in my gut, readying to explode. My vision pulses and the room tilts.

I'm going to retch.

I race down the hall to the bathroom just in time to flip the toilet seat up before gagging. Tears sting as my stomach empties, matching every other ounce of my body.

The room spins around me as I sit back on my heels, wiping my mouth with my sleeve. Sweat beads on my brow as minutes pass. Muffled sounds from the TV are audible, but none of the words register.

Getting up from the floor, I rinse my mouth and wash my hands, splashing my face before heading back down the hallway.

Just as Marlys comes back into my line of sight, the doorbell rings.

She meets my gaze. She's not just sad, she looks terrified. Of what, though? Who is she expecting?

A weird, unsettled feeling creeps over me, but I push it down.

"It's probably Xander," I say, trying my best to reassure her.

Marlys goes to the door, her fingers rest on the knob— one second, two, three—then finally opens it. I couldn't have been more wrong.

It's not Xander. It's not any neighbour. It's them.

Two police officers stand on the doorstep—one man, one woman—both in crisp navy uniforms. Their straight postures and stern expressions give nothing away, gaze flicking between Marlys and me.

"Mrs Brannigan?" the male officer asks.

"Yes?" She sniffles and wipes her nose with a tissue from the sofa table.

"I'm Detective Sergeant Rowan Pike, and my colleague here is Detective Constable Sienna Kaur. May we come in?"

The officers follow her into the lounge room and she mutes the TV. She waves an arm toward the couch, and they take a seat at one end, while Marlys sits two seats away.

"Is this about Hunter?" Marlys asks, briefly glancing at the TV before returning to the officers.

"Yes," Pike says.

"Is it really him?" Marlys asks through sobs.

"At this stage, we can't verify the identity of the remains. However, given that your husband was a well-known public figure, we wanted to speak to you directly before the coroner does his part."

"Was?" I say, speaking up. I shift closer to Marlys. "I thought you said you couldn't be certain, but you're already referring to him in the past tense."

Pike shifts in his seat and clears his throat. "Like I said, he was—sorry, is—well known."

I frown at him and glance over at Detective Constable Sienna Kaur, trying to make sense of it all. So Marlys doesn't need to ask the questions that must be burning inside of her, too.

"To formerly identify the remains, we need a family member to come down to the morgue," the female officer says. She's softly spoken, and it's clear she's trying to be sympathetic.

"I'll do it," I say, tapping Marlys on the shoulder.

"No," Marlys says, turning to me. She shakes her head. "You shouldn't have to see him like... that."

"Really, it's fine. Besides, you have enough on your mind right now. Let me do it."

Detective Pike cuts back in. "That's noble of you, young man, but how old are you?"

"He's sixteen," Marlys says in a whisper. "Too young, right?"

He nods. "That's correct. You need to be eighteen at least. I'm sorry, but Marlys, we need to ask you to come instead."

She lets out a shaky breath and nods. "I'll do it."

17

———————————————

THE SHELL OF A MAN

MARLYS

The plush covering of Xander's front passenger seat is like butter against my skin, yet my mind reels of what I'll be walking into. If only I could stay in this little capsule, protected from the world outside this glass and metal contraption.

But I know it needs to be done.

Xander turns off the engine and places a warm hand over mine. "You okay?"

I'm not. He's just trying to do his job as my support person. The police officer said I could bring with me. There's nothing he can say to make this better—we both know that.

"Yeah," I say with a nod.

Cracking open the car door, Xander races around, opening it fully like the gentleman he is. Flashing a weak smile, I climb out, straightening my dress, readying myself. I can't move, can't bring myself to face this——to see what's left of my husband.

"Marlys?" Xander says, pulling me from my thoughts.

"I'm not sure I can do this." My eyes are precariously damp, but I blink, forcing them back.

Xander grabs hold of my hand, edging me forward. "I've got you."

The next few steps are heavy and forced, like wading through ankle deep mud. He grips tighter, urging me to move on.

"Good afternoon," Xander says to the front desk. He places a hand on my back. "Marlys Brannigan," then lowers his voice. "She's here for... ugh, to meet with the coroner."

The clerk picks up the phone and speaks with someone. A moment later the Detective Sergeant Rowan Pike comes from the back.

"Mrs Brannigan, thank you for meeting me." He turns to Xander. "Please take a seat," he waves to two chairs by a water fountain. "This shouldn't take too long."

"He can't stay with me?" I ask, voice straining.

"This will only take a minute."

"It's fine, Marlys. I'll be right here when you get back," Xander offers.

I follow Pike through the door into a hallway, then into another room where the coroner waits.

"Thank you for coming so quickly. I'm sorry to meet you under these circumstances, Mrs Brannigan." I nod, blinking back the wet in my eyes. "I understand this must be difficult for you, but I need to prepare you for what you're going to see." He pauses, watching my response, then continues. "You husband sustained several injuries to his abdomen and head. Blood is present too. Are you comfortable proceeding?"

I definitely don't want to see him splayed out on a butcher block like a slab of beef.

"I'm ready," I lie.

He guides me into the next room, where a large pane of glass looks into another room. Stainless steel lines the walls and floor, with matching bench-tops. And a table in the centre when something large and uneven rests underneath a cover.

I gasp at the sight. "Is that...?"

Pike nods. "Yes."

On the other side of the pane, the coroner reappears. He confirms we're ready, then peels back the cover, down to the hips.

I can't help but stare, unmoving.

This isn't my husband.

This isn't Hunter.

It's not the man who sat at the dinner party, the one I cooked his favourite dishes for just so he could land his latest and greatest deal. And it's definitely not the man I first loved. The one whose eyes lit up every time I entered the room, and that gave me butterflies whenever his warmth touched my skin.

No, I don't know what this is.

It's the shape of a person, but there's nothing personable out it—about him. The greying skin resembles a decaying alien. Streaks of blood leak from two slits—one above the hip, and another just below the curve of its ribs. There's a split running diagonal over the forehead, raised and discoloured.

This isn't a man. This is a shell of a person.

Of... Hunter.

My mind goes back to that last kiss. The one at the end of the dinner party, before he went out. It had been so out of character for him—at least in recent times. My fingers fly to my lips, remembering the touch. Warm and soft, even loving.

Not like these lips before me now. A loveless shade of blue.

A single tear falls, rolling down my cheek. Then another, and another. Until so many roll out it becomes a stream.

Pike places one hand between my shoulders and passes a small box of tissues with his other hand. I take them, blowing my nose.

"I'm sorry to do this, Mrs Brannigan, but we need you to say whether this is your husband, Hunter Brannigan, or not."

Through sobs, I affirm what they are desperate to know. "Yes, it's him."

Pike nods to the coroner through the glass.

"Can I go now?" I ask.

"We need to discuss a few things first." He guides me out of the room and into another. "Please sit," he says, directing me to a chair on one side of the desk. He takes the seat opposite.

There's a knock on the door before it opens and the coroner walks in, taking a seat beside Detective Pike

"Mrs Brannigan, thank you for giving us a few more minutes of your time. We have concerns about the injuries Mr Brannigan has."

"Concerns?" I ask. Isn't the fact he's been murdered enough of a concern?

The coroner nods. "The lacerations on his abdomen, well, my preliminary assessment indicates they were sustained after he died."

I narrow my eyes on him, brow furrowing. "What do you mean?"

"It means those wounds didn't cause his death." He shakes his head. "No, nor did the head injury."

"How did he die then?"

"You might not have noticed, but his lips were a bluish colour."

"Yeah, I thought that was because he's, well... not breathing."

"Between that, and our initial toxicology reports, I suspect he was poisoned."

"Poison," I gasp, hand flying up to my mouth. "Oh, my God."

"Further tests still need to be processed before we know for sure."

The coroner leaves the room, with just me and Pike at the desk.

"Is that everything?" I ask, thinking about Xander still sitting out in the foyer.

"For now. But, Mrs Brannigan, we'll be in touch *soon*."

The way he says 'be in touch soon' turnings my stomach inside out. He didn't say anything about Hunter, just me.

His gaze lingers a little too long, like he's already made up his mind about my involvement in this crime.

Am I his suspect number one?

18

____

UNDER SCRUTINY

MARLYS

The drive home is silent, but I don't miss the glances Xander throws. I know he's trying to look out for me, to make sure I'm okay. Yet, it feels like I'm under constant supervision. Ignoring him, I stare out the window at nothing in particular. Anything to take my mind off the experience I just had.

But it's futile.

Hunter was poisoned.

Who would do that? No one I can think of. It's not like I've ever discussed the best way to murder someone.I just don't understand it.

Neither the head injury, nor the stab wounds killed him. But someone went to a lot of trouble to make it look like Hunter was attacked, when he'd already been dead, or dying.

The need to inflict such gruesome injuries when he was already dead, both baffles and sickens my stomach.

I need answers.

The police want suspects.

"You're quiet," Xander says, side eyeing me again. I

don't know how he can be so calm right now. Especially since I thought he and Hunter were friends. But then again, I haven't seen Kage shed a single tear yet, either.

"Sorry," I reply. It's all I can muster for a conversation right now.

"Do you want to talk about it?"

"I don't even want to think about it."

He's quiet for a moment, like he's trying to find the right words to say. "Try not to think about it, Marlys. It'll just give you nightmares."

What a strange thing to say. But then, I suppose he's right. I shuffle in my seat, turning slightly to face him.

"It was awful... seeing him laid out like that. I mean, who would do that to him?"

His hand rests on top of my thigh, squeezing it before re-gripping the steering wheel. "I don't know. Did the police say anything?"

"Not really. After I saw him, they took me to this room and spoke to me about his cause of death. But that's it. Nothing about the investigation."

Xander looks over at me with furrowed brows. "They questioned you?"

"It wasn't like that." I think back over the past half an hour, questioning their true intentions. The detective and coroner had both acted kindly, but then something was different when they told me about the poison. "Hmm, actually, they were. Pike did say they would speak to me again soon. You don't think I'm a suspect, do you?"

"What? No, of course not," he says, glancing over at me again before back at the road. "Why would you think that?"

"I've seen it on TV. They always suspect the spouse." Tears well, daring once more.

"That's just protocol. Honestly, stop worrying. No one

thinks you killed Hunter. I know you didn't." He grabs my hand, reassuring me. "You're going to be alright, I promise."

I nod, accepting his reassurance, hollow as it seems.

A short time later, we pull into Xander's driveway. He follows me back to my house.

"Are you hungry? I'm going to make a sandwich since we missed lunch," I say.

"Sure, I could eat," he replies as we reach the front door.

The TV is still playing in the lounge room when we get inside. I'm not sure if Kage is using it to distract himself, or if he truly doesn't care about his father's demise. But I resolve that as a problem to deal with later.

Throwing my bag over a dining chair, I head into the kitchen. Xander takes a seat at the table as if it's second nature to him. On the chopping block, I set out bread before grabbing ham and cheese from the fridge. When I spin back around, Kage stands by the kitchen island.

"Hungry?" I ask.

He just nods and sits at the table opposite Xander.

"So, did you do it?" Kage asks.

"Do what?" Xander replies, brows furrowed.

"The ID."

Xander shifts back, leaning in the chair. "Yeah, well, I couldn't go in, but Marlys did."

I cut each sandwich in half, placing them on three plates, and set them on the table, taking a seat beside Xander.

Kage picks up his sandwich. "It was him, then?" Kage asks, then takes a bite.

"It was," I say. My chest tightens at the memory of Hunter laid out on the stainless-steel table.

"Do they know who did it?" Kage asks, looking between Xander and me. Something feels off though, and I don't miss the fact he hasn't asked about his father's injuries or appearance. But then again, maybe he just doesn't want to know.

"Not yet, but the detective said they'd be around to ask some questions," I reply.

"Ok," Kage says, getting up from the table and returning to the lounge room, like I've just asked him if he has school tomorrow, or something equally as drab. I don't know what's got into him, but right now I have more pressing concerns to deal with.

I turn to Xander. "That was weird, right?"

He shrugs. "Everyone deals with grief differently. Maybe he still hasn't processed it as being real yet."

"I suppose that's true."

With a screech, I stand from the table, chair almost falling backwards, and clear the remaining dishes from the table.

"Coffee?" I ask.

"Please," Xander says.

A few minutes later, I return to the table, coffee in hand. Just as I'm about to sit, I feel a little craving and jump back up, heading to the pantry. Hidden behind a bag of flour, and rice, I retrieve my favourite packet of biscuits—TimTams. I grab them and head back to the table, placing the packet between us.

Sliding one from the packet, I chew both ends off, then use it as a straw. The chocolate biscuits melt with the warm drink, and I pop it in my mouth before it all falls apart and sinks in the cup. Sweet chocolate is the tiny bit of happiness I need.

Xander watches on in amazement, and laughs.

"Don't knock it 'til you try it," I say.

"No thanks," he says, patting his stomach.

"Come on," I nag.

"I can't say no to you, can I?" he says with a chuckle, taking one from the packet. "So, what's the trick?"

I take another biscuit. "Copy me."

The biscuit's halfway to my mouth—then the doorbell rings. Xander and I share a look. Really—the police are here so soon?

"Want me to get the door while you put those away?" Xander asks.

"If you don't mind. Thanks."

After cleaning away the mess, I head over to the front door, where Xander is speaking to Detective Sergeant Pike. He turns to me as I approach.

"Mrs Brannigan, do you have a moment to go over a few things?" Pike asks. Nodding, I move aside to allow them in. He scans the room as he enters, noticing Kage and the loud TV. "Is there somewhere a bit more private we can talk?"

"The kitchen?" I ask, waving towards it.

He shakes his head. "Somewhere without distractions, perhaps?"

"The rumpus room might work," Xander suggests.

The three of us head down the corridor to the rumpus room at the back of the house.

"Nice setup you have here," Pike comments, looking through the wall of sliding glass doors and out to the swimming pool and patio.

"We don't use it nearly enough. Will this work for you, then?"

"Yes. May I?" he says. I nod, and we all take a seat on the sectional.

Pike pulls out a navy-coloured notebook with the police insignia on the cover, flipping it open to a blank page. He jots something down, then sits back.

"Mrs Brannigan—"

"Please, just call me Marlys," I say.

He smiles. "Marlys. Today I need to ask a few preliminary questions for the investigation When was the last time you saw your husband, Hunter?" he asks matter-of-factly.

"It was the Friday night, after the dinner party."

"Did he say where he was going?"

"Yes, to Xander's house," I say, glancing at him.

He looks between us. "And you're Xander?"

He nods. "I am. My house is there." Xander points to his backyard, visible through the glass door.

"Right," the detective says, making a note. "And Marlys, did Hunter say what he was doing, or when he planned to be home?"

"It was work-related," Xander blurts.

Pike raises a hand. "Please, I need to hear these answers from Mrs—uh, Marlys. I will interview you in good time."

Xander frowns, but sits back on the lounge, folding his arms.

"Marlys?" he asks. "The question."

"Yes, he said he needed to get some business advice and that he would be home late."

"And do you know if he came home after that?"

I shake my head. "Honestly, after I cleaned up the kitchen, I went straight to bed, exhausted."

"When did you first notice Hunter *missing*?"

"The next morning, when I woke up. His side of the bed hadn't been slept in, and he wasn't asleep on the couch downstairs either, or in his home office."

"Okay," Pike says, jotting down more notes. When he's done, he looks back up, narrowing his gaze. "Can you tell me anything about Hunter's business?"

"No. He kept all of that to himself. Didn't like me meddling in that stuff."

"But you knew some of his business associates."

His words are more a statement than a question, and I don't know where this line of questioning is going. Or if it has any bearing on Hunter's situation.

"How do you mean?" I ask.

"Well, you hosted the dinner party, didn't you?"

"Yes," I frown. "Are you referring to Grayson?"

He nods. "Yes. Grayson Whitmore and Brielle Maddox."

"That was the first time I had met them, but I don't understand what you're getting at." I shift uncomfortably in my seat, and Xander raises a hand, rubbing my back. I glance at Xander, searching for answers. His mouth draws into a straight line, giving nothing away.

The detective's eyes narrow on me, and his voice changes, more curious. "Can you tell me about the relationship between Hunter and Brielle?"

"Relationship? Honestly, all I know is they mentioned a takeover at the dinner party, so I assumed Hunter was buying their business. I can't be certain, though." I glance at Xander again. "You probably know more about that than I do."

"Marlys," Pike says, lowering his voice. "We have reason to believe Hunter had a personal relationship with Ms Maddox."

For a moment, my mind searches for the meaning behind his words. My pulse rises, anxiety prickling in my chest.

"Personal relationship? They were friends."

He shakes his head. "No, more than that."

Warmth floods my cheeks, not out of embarrassment,

but from the anger that's building inside of me. "He was cheating?"

"It seems that way, yes."

I hold his stare for a long moment as my eyes become wet. Closing my eyes, I force them back, allowing my ire to build instead.

"I always suspected he was unfaithful, but Brielle... I welcomed her into my home, and... she... oh my God." Burying my face in my hands, Xander's warm hand rubs my back again, before wrapping around me.

"Can we wrap this up now?" Xander asks the detective. "Marlys has had a rough couple of days. She needs some time to process all of this."

"Just a few more questions and that'll be it," he replies.

Sitting back up, I say. "Let's get this over with, then."

He looks out to the garden. "Do you ever have problems with rodents around here?"

"Rodents—like rats and mice?" I ask, unsure where he's going with this.

"Yes, any infestations, etc."

I shake my head, trying to recall. "I wouldn't say 'infestation', but about three months ago we had field mice coming in through the laundry. We kept finding mice droppings on the tiles. Hunter was furious about it."

His brows shift high on his head. "How did you resolve it?"

"I didn't. Hunter did. Apparently, it's happened before, and he already had some rat poison sitting. So, he did whatever you're supposed to do with it, and... well, the mice stopped leaving their evidence."

"Has this got something to do with Hunter's death?" Xander asks.

Pike frowns. "The poison in Hunter's system was rat poison."

My mind reels at the revelation—I had access to the poison—I had motive. My heart pounds heavy in my chest, beating so hard it feels like it might explode.

"Surely you don't think I poisoned my husband because he cheated on me?" I blurt out.

He narrows his gaze and asks, "Did you?"

"Oh, my God. No, never. I couldn't."

With a snap, the notebook closes, and he stands. "Thank you for your time, Marlys. We may have more questions for you, so please ensure you're contactable."

I force a quick breath. "Are you telling me not to leave town? Like in the movies?"

He nods. "Something like that."

Then he just stares.

Not at Xander. Not outside at the pool. Not even at his notebook.

Just at me.

Like he's already decided I'm guilty.

19

OVERHEARD

KAGE

Last night was weird. Feverish dreams filled the little sleep I was lucky enough to get. *Again.* They've been more frequent since Dad's disappearance. Now he's gone, they're levelling up. Each one more disturbing, more confusing than the one before.

As usual, the woman appears as my mum, before twisting, contorting into the face of another. I still can't figure out who she is, though. My gut says I know her, but no matter how much I try to remember, I just can't.

I've started noticing other weird shit too. The drawer of my desk, where I hide her pictures—that was open this morning. So was my wardrobe. I'm certain they were closed when I went to bed last night. Maybe I'm wrong—they were already open, and I didn't notice amongst all the piles of dirty clothes and stuff. Have I been sleepwalking? Fidgeting with stuff, unaware.

I'm losing my damn mind.

Would it really be that surprising, given the bullshit I've dealt with in my life so far?

The thing that's worrying me more than anything, are

the whispers. Not all the time. Just now and then. So faint that I can't even be sure I heard them at all. At first, I thought Marlys had left the TV going. But it wasn't that. Then I considered my Xbox and gaming headset. Maybe I forgot to log off and my friends were still joking around. It wasn't that either.

I heard it again last night, in my dream. Whatever they said, I couldn't make out the words, yet the prickling anxiety, the urgency of it—that I can't stop feeling.

Before Xander went home last night, I overheard them talking. Apparently, the police grilled Marlys hard yesterday. They practically accused her of killing my dad.

She didn't, though.

They were also talking about Dad and Brielle. No surprise there. I didn't exactly know who he was cheating with, but my gut said he was up to something. And given what I heard Marlys say, she had no idea.

Shouldn't they interview me by now? I guess 'out of sight, out of mind' is true. No one pays me any attention. That's how I get away with what I do.

Since the cops knew about the affair, I assume they've spoken with them. Or at least Brielle. She's probably a suspect, too.

If she's not, she should be.

If the cops won't ask the right questions, then I will. And that little voice told me exactly where to start.

Grabbing my bag, I swing it over one shoulder and put my baseball cap on. Racing down the stairs, I head to the front door, ready to leave.

"Kage?" I hear Marlys call out. "Are you going somewhere?"

"Going to a mate's place," I call back to her.

She appears momentarily in the foyer. "It's not safe, Kage. Please stay home today."

"It's fine. Stop stressing out," I say, rolling my eyes.

"At least let me drive you"

"No!" I blurt, almost in a panic. I can't have her finding out what I'm up to. "I've got my phone. I'll call you if anything happens."

"And what if it's too late by then?"

"For fuck's sake, Marlys."

She huffs, struggling. "Well, what time will you be home?"

"I dunno."

I barrel out the front door and make a beeline for the bus stop at the end of the street.

I don't have plans with anyone. But I have a plan I want to put into action.

The bus pulls up a few minutes later, and I jump on board, sitting at the back. Half an hour later, I get off in the city centre, a block away from my destination. I can walk the rest of the distance. It'll be easier that way.

I don't give a shit about the investigation. Dad's dead, and that's that. But after overhearing Marlys and Xander talking about her interrogation, something still nags at me in my gut. Obviously, the cops are looking at people he was close to, and if they're not looking at me or Xander, then they've got to be closing in on his business associates.

Brielle Maddox and Grayson Whitmore.

Xander said dad was buying them out and with the affair in the mix, I bet Brielle's shitting herself. Grayson too. In all honesty, I couldn't care less about either of them. But I need to know who's going to crack first.

A woman like Brielle has secrets.

And if she wants to fuck things up, I have to be ready.

There's a coffee shop a few doors down from their business, *Whitmore and Associates*. I've seen them here before and hope I haven't wasted my time coming here today.

The memory of those urgent whispers along with my gut instinct compels me to continue. I pull my hoodie up and head inside, taking my place in the lengthy queue.

Right now, I'm just another guy in line for overpriced caffeine.

The overhead board displays a menu written in multicoloured chalk. I need to get something quick, or people will want to know what I'm doing. Glancing up, I stare at the menu as if I give a shit about any of it.

Two baristas flurry about behind large silver coffee machines. Rows of small, medium, and large disposable cups sit stacked on top. They jot abbreviations in black in on the lids and pass them to the cashier who calls out the orders.

"Order for Brielle. Order for Grayson."

I force myself not to react. *Stand still, pretend you didn't notice.*

But I didn't notice them, standing over to the side, waiting for their orders. How I missed that is beyond me. Yet, thanks to the cashier, I'm focussed on my subjects. Side eyeing them, they settle into a booth in the far corner, where only a few others are scattered around.

Finally, I place my order—something simple to speed up this shit show. I pay the cashier and grab the bottle of Coke, meandering inconspicuously to the adjacent booth. With my back to them, I sit behind Grayson, slithering down into the seat.

I pull out my phone, squish an earbud into one ear, and fake chilling out. Swiping to the recording app I downloaded on the way here, I click 'record' and listen with the bud-free ear.

Angry whispers pass between them. I strain to hear their conversation.

"The cops are trying to pin this on us," Grayson says. His voice is tight with barely controlled rage.

A feminine exhale comes next. It's Brielle. "They don't have anything," she says, calm and collected, like murder is no different from her business dilemmas.

"They know about the affair," he hisses.

"That doesn't mean anything," she says with confidence. She seems awfully relaxed for someone who could be facing twenty to life right now.

"Doesn't it?" Grayson asks, rhetorically. "They're digging into our finances, Brielle. They think we have something to gain here."

Brielle lowers her voice further, whispering quieter than before. "Well, don't we?"

Her calculating words make the hairs on my arms prickle.

Grayson lets out a bitter laugh. "We're fucking screwed, Brielle. Without him, the buyout won't happen. Isn't that the whole reason you–." He pauses, and I wish I could see the expression on their faces, so I could see what's not being said out loud. "The whole fucking reason you slept with him?"

"Lower your voice, Grayson," Brielle scolds.

"Are you fucking serious right now? Don't you see what's happening?"

"I understand perfectly, which is why you need to shut the hell up and let me handle this."

Grayson mutters something I can't hear. The seat behind me squeaks as he shifts in the leather seat.

Brielle continues. "They have nothing solid on either of us. Stay quiet and we'll be fine. It's that simple."

He sighs. "Yet."

I check my phone to ensure the recording is still working. It is. Then take a long sip of my Coke, celebrating this win.

This little outing has turned out far better than I imagine it would. And I've learned a lot more than anything Marlys could divulge. I guess my gut—or those whispers—were right.

Their conversation turns silent and for a minute I wonder if they've up and left without me realising. I sneak a sideways glance, but they're still there. Letting the recording continue, I wait a little longer, just in case. But they move on to less interesting topics. Sliding my finger over the recording, I stop and save it as a file before shoving it back in my pocket. I scull my Coke and check my watch like I've got somewhere pressing to be. Then I slip out of the coffee shop like I was never even there.

My sneakers beg to run once I reach the footpath, but I force myself to keep a regular pace.

At the bus stop, I sit, leaning against the frame, scanning the vicinity for signs of Brielle or Grayson. When the coast is clear, I pop my earbuds in both ears and return to the recording, listening from the start.

I have some juicy info. And I'm not sure what I'll do with it right now.

But I know one thing is for sure—Brielle and Grayson are lying about something.

20

SHIFTING TIDES

MIRANDA

He managed to drag himself away from her after Kage left this morning. It's surprising, since I was beginning to think he is permanently glued by her side. Pathetic. That kind of man—one that follows a woman around like a lost dog—he's no man at all.

For heaven's sake, have some damn pride.

But of course, Xander doesn't hear a word I say.

At least he's busying himself with something more, becoming of a man in his forties. He's been out in the sun half the day, mowing, raking, pulling weeds from between the plants in his herb garden. All things he's done before. But now he's messing around with planks of wood.

Since when has he fancied himself as a carpenter?

Perhaps he's trying to keep his mind off Hunter.

Though Marlys seems to be helping him out with that, whether she realises it or not.

At the very least, it's unsettling. That a woman widowed just days ago, now swoons over the neighbour. It's disgraceful, even with everything I know about Hunter's past.

She should be ashamed of herself.

And to think those two have been fawning over each other in front of my son. It's no wonder Kage hides himself away in that bedroom all the time. I fear, after everything he's been subjected to, he'll never know how to have a healthy relationship.

My heart swells at the thought. Missing him, the reminiscent pull to be around him.

He's been looking at my picture more often lately. On the one hand, I'm glad he has the reminder, but on the other, seeing him pine—so much angst and longing for the mother he can no longer have—it unravels me every time.

It's that bastard's fault.

And I'm glad he finally got what was coming to him.

Though now he's gone, I'm forever looking over my shoulder—just in case.

This life, or, whatever it is I'm doing now—it's a solitary existence. I don't remember seeing anyone like me before now, so even if Hunter turned up here, I'm not even sure I'd know.

I don't even want to think about him anymore. Yet, my replacement brings everything back—over and over again. Tormenting.

Maybe this is what purgatory feels like.

But what did I ever do that would warrant that?

I did my best. Tried to live a good life. Loved my family, cared for Hunter even when he didn't deserve it. But still, I'm tethered to this place. Even when I leave the corners of this space, like the times I've visited Amelia—it's like a rope, stretching, pulling, daring to snap, only to be yanked back again, rooted forever more.

There's some place better for me. Where I don't have to dwell on the past. I know the way, but Kage... Leaving him is out of the question. But even more than that, there's unfinished business that I don't know will ever be finalised.

Xander heads back inside the house, leaving the garden free from labouring sounds of the saw and hammer. We'd been here as a family before—back then—for barbecues and parties. Though the garden has advanced a lot since then, and it's obvious he takes a lot of care with it.

Moving closer to the half-built structure, he's built a hexagonal frame, though no floorboards have been nailed on yet. And tall square pillars of pine reach high at each corner.

A gazebo?

Marlys probably stirred this idea in him. Some sort of ridiculous romantic gesture intended to win her heart.

No one has ever done anything like that for me.

I shift closer. A magnetising pull gently guiding me.

Voices interrupt my inquisitive stare. Marlys and Xander are on the patio, mugs in hand. He settles on the patio swing, patting the seat beside him. She accepts his offer—oh so generous—so close their knees brush against each other.

Their laughter sickens me.

Unable to control my ire, I rush towards them, shifting around and through where they sit. Marlys shivers, and her hair flitters in the breeze.

"Did you feel that?" she says in a low voice, rubbing her upper arms with both hands.

"What? The breeze?" he asks.

She nods. "It was freakishly cold, don't you think?"

Xander laughs and wraps an arm around her shoulders, pulling her into him. She doesn't fight the embrace and tucks her head into his shoulder.

I rush around them, trying to pull them apart. To separate this abhorrence.

"There it is again," she whispers.

"It's just the seasons changing," he reassures her. "Summer is ending, it's coming into autumn. That's all."

She shakes her head. "I don't think so. It's the same as at my house–inside."

He rubs her arm, the one that's still wrapped around her tightly.

Marlys glances up at Xander. "I'm serious, Xander. My house is haunted, and I think yours might be too."

21

COERCED

MARLYS

The house smells like the laundry aisle at the supermarket, with pine blending with floral scents, with a clean, powdery finish. After the last few days, I've used every bottle, tube, and tub of cleaning products, just to keep myself from dwelling. On Hunter, on Amelia, the notes, the affair, and the angry haunting that's suffocating this house.

It's all I can do to prevent myself from falling off the edge where I'm teetering. A lifeline preventing my total collapse into insanity.

If only I'd had time for a hobby, like Xander, who's almost done with his garden project. Wiping the last drizzle of window cleaner from the dining room window, I catch a glimpse of him through the garden. He's so focused and content in his element. So free. Yet here I remain, a prisoner in my own life. Waiting for all of this to blow over. Then I can press reset and start again.

Loud thuds rap against the door, stern and urgent. My pulse rises along with it. At the door stand the two police officers who were here only days ago.

"Mrs Brannigan," Detective Sergeant Rowan Pike says. His voice is lower, more solemn than when he was last here, almost lowering another octave.

That can't be good.

"Detectives," I say, though the greeting is weak. "Is there an update? Did you find the killer?"

He frowns. "May we come in?"

I pull the door open wider and wave an arm, ushering them inside to the lounge room. Each of us settle on the couch.

"So," I say, watching them pull out their notepads and pens. "How is the investigation going? Please tell me you've found Hunter's... uh..." My words trail off, but I'm confident they get my meaning.

"His toxicology report came back and it was positive for a chemical called brodifacoum." He pauses for a moment, holding my gaze, but I just wait, eager to know all the details. "It's a rodenticide, more commonly known as 'RatSack'."

My hands fly to my mouth, gasping. "RatSack? Are you sure?"

"Yes, Mrs Brannigan. Science doesn't lie." His eyes narrow. "But people do."

Those words, and the look on his face is unnerving. Surely he isn't saying what it sounds like. Last time they were here, they asked about rodent problems, and without a second thought, I'd handed them myself on a silver platter. And now, the toxicology report had given them more reason to think I'm a cold blooded killer.

A lump forms in my throat. I can't respond. But even if I wanted to, what could I even say to change his mind?

Detective Constable Sienna Kaur speaks, but Detective Pike continues staring at me like I'm under the spotlight now. "The thing is Mrs Brannigan, poisoning as a method of homicide, mostly used by women."

My heart beats faster, banging against my ribs, yearning to jump right out of my body.

She shifts back in her seat, propping her notebook on her knee. Her voice softens, and she locks eyes with me, but this time, it's less accusatory. More like empathy, or even sympathy.

"Did you ever fear your husband, Mrs Brannigan?"

"I'm not sure I know what you mean," I reply.

"Did he ever hurt you?" Kaur clarifies.

I shake my head. "No, never. Hunter wasn't like that. I mean, sure, he got angry sometimes, but he never hit me. If that's what you want to know."

The detectives note a few words in their pads, then return their focus to me. "Did he ever say hurtful things to you, call you names, put you down—that sort of thing?"

This line of questioning has nothing to do with Hunter's murder. My mind rattles, trying to make sense of it. But at the same time, I'm scouring memories to find the answers, too.

My head tilts to the side. "No, not really."

Kaur's eyes narrow, and she chews on the end of her pen, then drops it to her lap. "Marlys, can I call you that?" I nod. "Can you tell me what Hunter was like at home?"

"Well," I begin, eyes darting to the ceiling. I wish I knew what they wanted me to say instead of these odd questions.

"Let's start from the beginning," Detective Pike interjects, forcing my attention back to him.

I nod. "I can do that."

"How did you and Hunter first meet?" he says.

"It all started about a year and a half ago. Or maybe a little bit before that." I shake my head. "That doesn't matter, though. I had recently lost my job, so I signed up to a temp agency. You know, typing, filing, answering phones—that sort of thing. Well, I had just finished my first six-week contract, and I needed my next gig. They didn't have any block contracts available, but they had some relief work available. I was broke with next to no savings in the bank, so I jumped at the chance. It ended up being at Brannigan Enterprises. My job was pretty much helping out his admin or receptionist—whatever you want to call it. She was swamped with paperwork that Hunter just slapped on her desk. Anyway, after about a month, she took annual leave, and I backfilled her position. So naturally, Hunter and I began interacting more often. From the first day I was there, I thought he was handsome even though he's older. A silver fox, you might say, like George Clooney, or whatever. I never in a million years thought he'd reciprocate the interest. But he did. The more we interacted, our conversations grew form a few words, to sentences, then he started asking me to stay back late—paid me overtime and everything—to help him with all these meetings and deals he was pushing through, trying to expand the business."

I pause for a minute, recalling back then. It hadn't been that long ago, but still it feels like a hundred years has passed. And thinking of that Hunter, back then, makes me long for my husband.

"Anyway, one night we were there quite late. My stomach actually rumbled in front of him. I was mortified but he just laughed it off and offered to buy me dinner. Not much was open, but a late-night convenience store. He grabbed a bagful of stuff and drove me to the mountain. You know, the one that overlooks the town. When we got there, he laid out this whole picnic type dinner on the sightseeing deck, overlooking the lights. It was magical." I sigh, wiping the corner of my eye where a tear threatens to fall.

"From that moment, I was under his spell. Things went hard and fast. He took me out every other night—dinner, movies, galas, parties. And bought me so many gifts. After a few months, he proposed. I thought it was too soon, but Hunter—well, he said he knew what he wanted, and he didn't want to waste another day without it. Me. You see, he completely swept me off my feet."

I stand from the seat. "I need a glass of water. Would either of you like something?"

Both Pike and Kaur decline my offer, and I head to the kitchen. Still, the memories flood my mind. A tear escapes falling down my cheek. Splashing cool water over my face, I pour my glass of water and head back to the lounge room.

"Better?" the Kaur asks.

"Yes, much," I say with a weak smile. "So where were we? Okay, right. Our wedding—after the honeymoon, that's when things changed, I suppose. But I've talked to others and apparently that's quite normal. Goodbye fairy tale, hello married life."

Pike's mouth twitches at the corner, a sly grin forming. "Ain't that the truth?" he says humorously. Kaur scorns him, and I wonder if they're 'together'. I brush it off. It doesn't matter.

"Marlys," she starts. "When you say things changed after you got married, what exactly do you mean?"

Sucking in a deep breath, I let it whoosh out, shoulders slumping. "Well, for one thing, I had no idea how to be a wife... or a stepmother, for that matter. Both were steep learning curves. I'm still trying to figure out this whole parenting thing with Kage. He's sixteen so..."

"Teenagers are the worst," Pike mumbles with a chuckle.

"Don't get me wrong. I love him in my own way. It's just really hard to love someone who hates you."

They both nod like they understand, maybe even pity me. But I don't want their pity. I want answers. To get them, I need to get this interrogation out of the way so they can be done with focusing on me and start focusing on the real killer.

"Can you go back to Hunter for a second?" Kaur asks.

"Yeah. Sorry, sometimes I get sidetracked. Look, Hunter is—was—this high-profile business executive. He was super busy all the time. When he came home, he just wanted to relax and unwind. He had a routine that he adhered to, and I was the newcomer in the family, so I needed to figure out how to maintain that."

"Would you say he was controlling, then?" she asks.

I cringe at the word. Hunter hated it when I accused him of that. He'd roll over in his grave—not that he had one yet—still laying on that stainless steel tray in the coroner's office.

"A little bit."

A rush of cold air breezes through the room, ruffling the stray strands of my hair. Glancing up at the air conditioning unit, it's off. The TV remote, sitting on the edge of the coffee table, drops to the floor beside my foot. A shiver runs down my spine, shoulders shivering. But my pulse rises, heart pounding—not just from the police interrogation—but because I know she's here right now. Watching, waiting. Hearing me talk about my relationship with Hunter. What she must think of me in this moment.

I laugh weakly, but words fail me. There's no point telling them the house is haunted. That Hunter's ex-wife is hovering in this space alongside the three of us. They'd just drag me off to the looney bin. Wouldn't they?

"Marlys, do you know what coercive control is?" Kaur asks, leaning towards me.

Shaking my head, I still can't find the right thing to say.

"Coercive control is a type of domestic abuse," she says, watching me closely.

I recall the posters I'd skimmed over the day I went to the police station. "Like domestic violence?"

"Yes, that's exactly what it is, Marlys. Coercive control is just one type, just like physical abuse, or emotional abuse."

I understand the premise of what she's saying. Yet, I know very little beyond that. I frown. "I'm not sure I understand why you're bringing this up?"

"Did Hunter ever threaten you? Or maybe he tried to embarrass you in front of others?"

I shake my head. "I don't think so."

"Did he ever try to intimidate you?"

"Uh," I say, but it's all I can force myself to say. I think back to all the times his tone and demeanour felt like a scolding. That's what she's talking about. But I shouldn't talk ill of the dead. Especially being my husband. Her brows raise high on her forehead like she's reading my mind.

"Everything they do is about control. Threats, humiliation, intimidation—it's all intended to harm or punish, or even just to frighten them into obedience."

Kaur pauses for a few seconds, and I suspect she's trying to see if I give anything away with my body language. I stiffen, being mindful not to do anything that might feed their story.

Her voice lowers as she continues. "Marlys, in marriages... like yours... they isolate you from your family and friends. Turn children against their other parent, or... stepparent." Tilting her head, I read between the lines. She believes Hunter was like these other men she's describing. A monster behind a mask. I remain silent as she explains further. "Do you know what gaslighting is?"

"Kind of," I say. I've heard the phrase before, but I can't say I truly know the definition or meaning.

She sighs and smiles weakly. There's that pity again. Of course she thinks I'm one of these victims. I'm not. But then again, memories shuffle through like a photo album. Every tear he caused, every pain I'd endured. Every dying day of solitude.

Maybe there's something to their suspicion.

My stomach twists at the thought. Wouldn't I know if I were a victim of DV?

"These guys—they make you doubt yourself, your experiences. Even your own sanity. They aren't good guys, Marlys. But they groom you so you never see it coming. Not until it's too late."

Something in my chest swells. Not love. Like when you're young and you lose your first love. It's agony, and without the coping skills to work through it, all you're left with is a feeling of drowning in grief and sorrow.

"Marlys, who controlled the finances in your marriage?"

I push a stray strand of hair behind my ear, avoiding her gaze. "Hunter did."

"And you were just expected to do all of this housework?" Kaur waves an arm around the vast home.

"Yes, but I wasn't working."

She shakes her head. "That's not the point, Marlys. Does any of this resonate with you?"

I shrug and slouch over further. I cant bring myself to

say what she clearly wants me to say. Or to admit the truth of it to myself.

Kaur shuffles over on the couch, closing the gap between us, and places one hand on my forearm as if we're friends. "Did Hunter ever hurt you or control you... sexually?"

The shock hits me, like a firm blow to the gut. Instinctively I look up, meeting her eyes. She knows he did, but I never told her. Maybe she's bluffing, hoping I'll walk into her trap.

"It's alright, Marlys," she almost whispers.

It feels strange, and awkward. This police detective inching up to me, almost consoling. It's a far cry from the brush off I received from the police when I tried to report Hunter missing.

Words evade me, though the tears welling in the corner of my eyes give me away. My gaze falls to the floor, staring at my bare feet. I should've put shoes on, but I didn't think I'd need to. But now my toes, with their pink gel polish, are out in the open, for anyone who pays an ounce of attention, to see.

Just like my emotions. The wall I'd built, crumbles one brick at a time, as they chip away with their chisel of questions—accusations.

"I think *you are* a victim in all of this Marlys. That Hunter groomed you and took you for granted. That he hurt you in many of the ways I mentioned. That's right, isn't it, Marlys?"

I start to shake my head, but Hunter's gone. There's no need to pretend anymore. My shake shifts to a nod. Small, and barely there, but a nod all the same.

Kaur pats my arm. "And you had enough. Finally hit your breaking point. Didn't you?"

My shoulders shrug, but I remain silent. Her question is rhetorical anyway.

"You needed to protect yourself. And Kage. And so, you decided to do something about it, and poisoned him."

Realisation dawns. I shake my head, over and over. "No, no, no. I didn't. I swear."

"The thing is, we've spoken with others who were close to Hunter and you. We know how he treated you. It's understandable, that you reached the end of your tether, and with no family or friends around to talk you, you did the only thing you knew to escape."

My head hangs heavy, both hands on top of my head. I shake my head again. This can't be real. They can't honestly think I did this.

I look up at Kaur. "Who..." I stutter. "Who did you speak to?"

"That doesn't matter. The point is, we understand. But Marlys, you can't just take the law into your own hands. I feel for you, I do, but a crime has been committed here, and justice has to be served."

"Yes, justice... but you've got the wrong person," I say, voice shaking.

"Let's move on for a minute, shall we," Pike says, throwing a look at Kaur. "Can you tell us about the relationship between Hunter and his son, Kage?"

"What about it?" I say, almost whispering. I try to steady myself, swiping the tears from my cheeks. Reaching over to the coffee table, I pull a tissue from the box, and blow my nose, crumpling it in my hand. I hold it tightly, like it's the only lifeline I have left right now.

"Did they get along?"

"Not really," I say. "Hunter is—was—quite strict. He

had rules and expectations. Kage is a teenager; he doesn't like being told what to do. But what teen does?"

"Did they get into arguments or fight?"

"Sometimes they argued, but Kage just goes to his room or goes to a friend's place. I'm the one left walking on eggshells, trying to navigate the house around them. They're both hot headed."

"And the night of the dinner party. Was Kage there too?"

"No, it was a business dinner. Kage never attended those—Hunter didn't want him there to embarrass him, and Kage thought they were pretentious. He was in his room all night, probably on his Xbox like he does most nights."

"Did you speak to Kage after the dinner party?"

"No, I don't think so."

"So, you can't be sure he was still at the house, then?"

I tilt my head a little. "Well, when you put it that way, I suppose not. But... surely you don't think Kage has anything to do with his father's murder, do you?"

Pike narrows his gaze. "We're still pursuing all avenues of enquiry right now. Having said that, it's not outside the realm of possibility either."

"No, you're wrong." I shake my head again, and my neck is starting to ache from repeating the movement so many times through this conversation.

"That may be so, but we'll still need to speak with him. Is he here now?"

"He's upstairs, I think."

Pike nods. "We'll need a guardian to join him because of his age, but we'd prefer it not be yourself. It might sway him from speaking openly."

"I can ask Xander," I say.

"Speaking of your neighbour, how close was he with Hunter?"

"They're friends. From what I know, they have been ever since they've been neighbours."

"How long might that be?" he asks.

"Hazarding a guess, at least sixteen years since Kage grew up in this house. But other than that, I really can't say."

"Have they ever had a falling out?"

He's not serious. They just accused me of murder. Then raise doubt about Kage. And now, Xander. This is outrageous, though a bit of relief sparks in my chest—they're investigating, so maybe there are others they're looking into as well.

"Not that I know of."

Pike jots a few things in his notebook, then glances back up at me again. "Did Hunter ever loan Xander money?"

I frown at him. "Money? I doubt it. Xander's in early retirement."

"Perhaps Xander resented Hunter?" he asks.

My brows pull together. "What on earth would he resent Hunter for?"

"Or maybe it was jealousy." He pauses for a second. "I believe you and Xander are quite close, aren't you?"

"We're friends. If you're suggesting I was unfaithful to my husband you're barking up the wrong tree. Hunter was the cheater—you told me that, remember?"

A smirk twitches at the corner of Pike's mouth. "Indeed."

They're doing it again. Taking something small and twisting it, stretching it, and pressing until the truth fits *their version* of events.

Kaur, who's been patiently observing the interrogation, shifts in her seat. "Could it be that Xander was protective of you, and had a falling out with Hunter about how he treated you?"

My mind flashes back to coffee on Xanders couch, and how he said if I wasn't happy, I should leave. And that I didn't need to put up with Kage's disrespect, either. But those are the words of any good friend.

I consider it for a moment. "No, Xander knows the 'professional' Hunter, not the one behind closed doors. Not the one I knew. Besides, shouldn't you be looking into Brielle and Grayson?"

"We've spoken to them both," Pike says. "And we'll be following up with them again soon."

"You found something?" I ask.

He nods. "All I can say right now is their financial situation is interesting, and we're digging into any potential motives either of them may have had."

"Good," I blurt. "Now, are we done here?"

"Just about," he says. "Though there's still the matter of Kage's interview." He looks at Kaur. "Let's get lunch, then swing back around?" She nods in agreement. Then he turns back to me. "If you can arrange for Xander to accompany Kage for the interview while we're gone, please."

I huddle them both towards the front door, hovering there in the doorway, watching them leave. My head and body are exhausted already. My gaze follows them down the street until they're no longer in sight. I take a step back inside, about to close the door, when I notice something out of place.

An envelope.

Sticking out from underneath the doormat.

I bend down and pull it out. It's just like the previous notes addressed to Hunter. But this time, the script on the envelope has a different name.

Mine.

22

———

DEMANDS

MARLYS

With news of Hunter's death engulfing the media, I believed the notes would stop. Their ominous nature was intended solely to force Hunter into action.

I was wrong.

I stare at the envelope in my hand. Same colour paper, same black script. With one glaring difference. Instead of Hunter's name, mine is plastered there. How they knew it, I don't know. And why they're writing to me now... well, all I can think of is they need me in his absence.

But what assistance could I possibly be?

If I opened it, I'd know. Yet something stops me. Fear, or dread. Or maybe it's the secret, daring to be known. I'm not sure I'm ready for more. It's like each new thing I learn, another blow to the memory of my marriage. To who I believed my husband was.

Pulling my phone from my pocket, I hit 'call'. It rings four times before he answers.

"Xander, I need you. Right now." The words come out

heavy and anguished, matching the feeling in the pit of my stomach.

"Is everything alright?" he asks.

I shake my head as if he can see it. "No, not even a little bit."

He sighs and I second guess whether I'm bothering him. I've relied so much on him since Hunter's disappearance, and then after his body was found. Maybe it's too much for him.

"I'm just in the garden finishing up the gazebo. Come through the side gate."

Despite my doubts, I shut the door behind me and head over, through the side gate to his backyard. The structure has come together so fast, but looking at the almost finished product, I can imagine how it'll look with seating and plants hanging from the rafters. Will he plant flowers around the edge where naked rows of earth sit right now? It's a beautiful sight, but even more so is his shirtless torso. A mix of sweat and dirt glisten under the midday sun, tinged pink from sunburn.

For a moment, the heavy feeling in my stomach changes to butterflies. Curling around my insides, with their anticipating caress. I move closer, where he's crouched at the gazebos entrance, where he's nailing the final handrail into place.

With one hand—the one without the envelope —I lean forward, touching his shoulder. He jumps, almost spinning, then stands.

"Shit Marlys, you scared me. Why didn't you say anything?"

There's no chance I'll admit to the truth. Especially since this view, from the front, is even more distracting.

"Sorry, I didn't mean to. You didn't hear the gate when I came in?"

He shakes his head. But then his gaze fixes on my hand. "Is that another one?"

I nod. "I haven't opened it."

He wipes his forearm over his face, clearing the sweat. "Let's go inside."

A few minutes later, we settle on the couch, side by side. Though I swivel to face him. "You don't mind opening it again?"

"Of course not," he replies, plucking it from my hand.

Just like last time, he slides a finger under the flap, tearing it open along the seam, before pulling out the folded paper from inside. My pulse rises as he scans the page. He frowns, then glances up at me, then rereads it again shaking his head.

"What's it say?" I clasp my hands together.

He clears his throat and sits up straighter like he's about to narrate a novel. "It says – I know you saw her. You were there. Stop hiding her from me. Let me see my sister." Xanders brows pull together, and holds my stare. "What the hell does that mean, Marlys?"

My gaze drifts to the ceiling as I try to put the pieces together.

He saw me.

His sister.

My mind races, grasping for anything. All I can think of is the incident at the care home. Amelia is there, it's where Hunter placed her. And if I'm being honest with myself, he was hiding her. If he hadn't died, I still wouldn't be any the wiser. Still, I have no knowledge about any family she might have.

The man—the angry one, who made a scene—who tried to attack me. I shake my head at the thought.

"What is it?" Xander asks.

I'd momentarily forgotten he was there. He doesn't know I went to see her. "Amelia."

"Amelia?" He shakes his head, scrunching up his nose. "What's she got to do with this?" He holds the note up between us.

"I think," I pause, trying to find the right words. "Well, I think I know who wrote the notes."

"What do you mean?" He asks, voice tightening. "What aren't you telling me?"

My shoulders shrug slightly, and I give a weak, sheepish grin. "I, uh, went to see her."

"You what?" he blurts, then runs a hand down his face.

Quietly, I sit, waiting for him to process the revelation.

"And you spoke with her?" he asks, lowering his voice.

I nod. "Just for a few minutes."

His gaze narrows as he calms himself. "What did she say?"

"Not much. Just that she has an... injury. And, well she mentioned someone else... someone called Miranda."

Xander's eyes grow darker, jaw clenching. "Who's that?"

"Apparently, she's a ghost."

"A ghost?" He mimics, then his shoulders loosen a little, and he relaxes. "Geez, Marlys. Your house isn't haunted. I told you that before."

I frown at him. "How do you know? Have you ever had a paranormal experience?"

"No. And neither have you. Because ghosts aren't real." He rubs the back of his neck. "Anyway, what's that got to do with the note."

"There was a guy, when I was leaving," I say, fidgeting with a hangnail. "He made a huge scene, then went outside. And... he tried to chase me."

"Oh my God, Marlys. And you're just telling me this now?" He balls his fists, banging them against his knees. "How do you expect me to keep you safe if you keep things from me?"

"I'm sorry, Xander. I didn't think about it like that. I got away in time, he didn't do anything to me."

"The thing is Marlys, if he is the guy, he knows where you live. How do you think you got this note? There's no postage stamp, and the mailman doesn't hand deliver to your doorstep."

He's right. I hadn't thought this through at all. Thank goodness Xander's making me realise this now. He does know where I live, and my car. He's followed me on—who knows–how many occasions? Dread pits in my stomach. How many times had he been close enough to hurt me and I hadn't known?

Tears sting, and my throat chokes on the words that I fail to push out. He shifts closer, wrap his arms around me.

"Shh, now. It's Okay," he says. I lean into his embrace, letting the tears falls onto his shoulder. One arm releases, and he drapes a hand over my hair, tucking it behind my ear. "You need to tell the police about this," he says. I shake my head, pulling back from him.

"No, I can't," I say. "That's the other thing I need to talk to you about. They interrogated me this morning... for hours, Xander. They think I did it."

"They what?"

"They asked me all sorts of questions. About Hunter–how we met, what our relationship was like," I lower my voice, "And DV."

"DV?" He starts, brows pulled together aggressively, but I cut him off.

"That's not all though. They also asked about you and Kage. They're coming back to interview him soon. I can't be with him; they won't let me. But I was hoping you might."

"Wait, what? They're interviewing Kage. Is he a suspect?"

"I'm not sure. They're interviewing everyone who was close to Hunter. They said they've already been to see Brielle and Grayson, too."

He frowns. "Well, those two–that makes sense, but Kage, I don't believe it."

"How do you mean 'those two make sense'?"

"Grayson and Hunter, have history. They started Brannigan Enterprises together. Though I doubt Hunter would ever have admitted that to anyone."

That can't be true. Hunter had never mentioned Grayson before the dinner party. But then I recall his introductions. Xander had met him before. He'd said as much, hadn't he? Something feels off and I can't put my finger on what that something is.

Xander takes in a deep breath, and blows it out slowly. "If anyone had a reason to want Hunter dead, Grayson did. He lost everything to Hunter. He really did a number on his so-called best friend."

"They really were close?"

He nods. "About as close as two men can be. But Hunter got greedy, practically stole Grayson's share."

"And Brielle?" I ask. "She was having an affair with him... maybe even loved him." I cringe at the thought, and nausea fills my stomach.

"Maybe she got sick of being the second woman. Or maybe he tried to call it quits. I can only speculate, Marlys, but what if she's hiding the temper of a scorned woman behind all that professional demeanour of hers? I don't think she's quite what she portrays herself to be."

He's right, of course. She did come into my home acting so nice and friendly. All the while she was cavorting with my husband behind my back. I can't even imagine how callous a woman has to be to pull that off as well as she did. Just the picture of her in my mind makes my heart pound, pulse beating faster, raging. I can't take it anymore.

Fury fuels my temper, that I'd pushed back for so long. Unable to control it any longer. I want to giver her a piece of mind. I want to call her out. My teeth clench together, grinding against each other.

I need to know if she did it.

If she's a murderer.

23

―――――

RECKONING

MARLYS

Leaving Kage in Xander's capable hands, I head for Whitmore and Associates. I drive as if on autopilot, everything else fading while my fury grows wilder with each passing minute. I've spent too much time at the mercy of others, and I choose Brielle to start my reckoning with. Though a small voice, in the shadows of my mind, whispers to me. It tells me I don't have it in me, to confront someone like her. That I'm only going to make a fool of myself, like some sort of unhinged idiot.

I have to do this. She has the answers I want. That I need.

Parking outside the building, my pounding heart hurries me to lock the door and head in.

Do it now. Before you lose your nerve.

With one swift movement, I grab the door handle and pull it towards me, making a bee line for the receptionist desk. I tower over her seated in the centre, as she glances up with a wavering smile. Though it disappears as fast as it came, and a frown emerges.

"Are you alright, miss?" she says.

In my rush, I didn't bother to spruce myself up, so I look like a hot mess. It doesn't matter. I don't need to exude some pretentious persona. Ignoring her concern, I press my intention.

"I need to see Brielle Maddox. It's urgent."

My nails rap against the desk, while she checks a calendar on her computer.

"I'm sorry, Ms Maddox is otherwise engaged. I have a 10am for tomorrow if you'd like?"

I shake my head, furiously. That won't do. "No, I need to see her—now." I nod towards the phone on her desk. "Tell her it's Marlys Brannigan."

The woman raises a single eyebrow but picks up the phone anyway. "Ms Maddox, sorry to bother you. There's a Marlys Brannigan here for you." She pauses, listening. I strain to hear, shifting a little closer, but only murmurs of words are audible. The woman nods her head. "Yes, Ms Maddox. I told her that, but..." She stops speaking, like she's been cut off.

I slap a hand a top the desk. "Which way is her office?"

She rises to her feet, still holding the phone to her ear. "I'm sorry, please. Just wait a moment." But I have no more fucks to give today.

Shifting around the desk, I head towards the offices in the back. Pulse beating faster with each step, until I see the name on a gold rectangular plaque, 'Brielle Maddox'.

I almost trip over my feet, but I reach the door. I grab the handle and turn. The door swings open. A large sleek desk is centred in the room, and a large painting that must've cost a pretty penny, covers half the wall behind her. The room is perfectly aligned, not a pencil out of place. Just like the woman behind the desk.

Her perfect, shiny hair has been pulled into a tight bun.

Not a single stray hair to speak of. And her make up screams business mogul, with a thick layer of crimson red painted on those lips. The ones that frame a perfect, broad white smile, like she's appearing on a toothpaste commercial.

"Marlys," she says. Her voice is as smooth as I remember it from the dinner party. Like she could tame a wild cat just by purring her words at it. "What a nice surprise."

"Cut the bullshit, Brielle," I blurt. But surprisingly, her perfected charade doesn't falter. Not even a little bit. Then I see it. Her smile punctuates with a tiny quiver at one corner, as it pulls into a half smirk. I'm not deterred, as it spurs my rage on, like accelerant to the flames–the one's metaphorically leaping from every inch of my skin. Daring to lash out at her, to burn a hole in that pretence, to bring everything that is Brielle Maddox to ashes.

She waves a hand towards a chair opposite her, on the other side of the desk. "Please, sit."

I hadn't noticed the receptionist catch up to me, but she's standing in the doorway, mouthing apologies to this vixen. She nods that it's okay, but the concern on the woman's face tells me that she's in for some serious punishment when I'm done here. A small spark of pity, for the woman emerges, like water dousing those flames in my heart. But I can't allow that. Not now.

I shift closer to Brielle, leaning both hands on her desk, narrowing my eyes. "What did you do?"

"Whatever do you mean?" she says. She rolls her chair backwards, and crosses her long, elegant legs, placing one hand on each arm rest.

"Don't act like you're so sweet and innocent," I say, hands on hips. "You were screwing my husband. I can't believe I welcomed you into my home, and all the while..." I let my words trail off. We both know exactly what I'm accusing her of. I suck in a long breath. "And now he's dead. So, tell me. What did you do?"

She leans back in her chair, crossing her arms as her eyes scan over me. If my accusation bothers her, she's not giving it away. The way her face is unmoving, lacking any sort of emotion, well, it's like she's made of metal–like a robot, without a heart.

Brielle breathes in through her nose, chest rising as she does, then exhales slowly. "Marlys," she starts. Her voice is measured, and while it's still smooth as the A-line dress she's wearing, there's an edge to it, like she's trying to maintain her control. "You're upset, I get it. You just lost your husband." She tilts her head, flashing that insufferable smirk. "But let's not pretend you're actually mourning him."

Her accusation is a slap in the face.

My hands curl into fists, and a rumble in my throat–a sound I've never heard from myself before–emits, low and furious. "How dare you."

A single shoulder rises. "Am I wrong?"

I can't stand this exchange any longer. I came here for answers, and instead she's flipping this back onto me, twisting everything–just like the police did.

"I know what you were doing. You thought you could take everything. His money, his name, my life as his wife. You couldn't handle being second, so you decided to get rid of him, didn't you?"

Her smile falters, finally. I've got her now. Then a frown forms, and for the first time since I stormed into this office, she's dropped the act.

"I didn't kill Hunter, and if you had a single ounce of common sense, you'd know why."

Knocking on the open office door causes our heads to swivel towards the inconvenient sound. Grayson.

My eyes narrow on him, and my heart roars with renowned rage. Does he know what she's done. But then I recall Xander saying he had just as much motive to get rid of Hunter. I take a quick step towards him but he ushers Brielle outside, closing the door behind him, leaving me alone in this sparse office. I consider jumping on her computer. To see if there's anything there. Maybe a calendar entry for the night Hunter disappeared–after the dinner party.

Hushed voices mumble outside the door, and I shift closer, placing my ear against it.

"Brielle," Grayson says in a stern low voice. "Give the woman some damn closure." He pauses for a second as she tries to resist, but he cuts her off. "Just make sure she doesn't go to the cops."

Closure. What the heck does that mean?

But a renewed sense of hope flickers in my mind. I knew they were hiding something. The question now is, are they going to divulge that to me. The simple fact that he's worried about the police finding out tells me it must be huge. Maybe they planned it together.

The door handle moves. My pulse races, bound to be caught standing here listening in. I take three long strides back to where I stood earlier, in front of the desk, just as Brielle glides in, back to her chair.

There's something different about her now, I realise. But I'm not sure what it is. She slides gracefully into her seat, crossing her legs again, before meeting my gaze.

"Sit down, Marlys," she says, but it's not commanding like earlier, more like defeat. I don't argue, and sit.

"Did you do it together?" I ask.

She scrunches up her face. "What? Murder?"

"Yes," I say matter-of-fact.

Brielle shakes her head. "No, Marlys. I didn't *kill* Hunter, and neither did Grayson." She inhales like she's searching for the words that might give me the 'closure' they whispered about. And for once her composed corporate appearance has an edge of discomfort. She picks up a pen resting on the desk and fidgets with it. "You've got it all wrong. To begin with, I *wasn't* in love with your husband."

I don't want to believe her, but in the cadence of her voice says she's being honest. But that doesn't mean the rest of my suspicions aren't right. It's not hard to imagine someone being with another for the sake of financial benefit. That's literally what the term 'gold diggers' means.

"I just want the truth, Brielle. I need to know what happened that night."

Her brows pull together. "I don't have the answer to that. After Grayson and I left your house, after dinner, he dropped me home, and he went to his house. I never saw Hunter again after that."

"And what about the affair? You knew he was married. Did you even think about me, or Kage, and how it might affect our family?"

She sits up straight in her chair, placing her hands back on the armrests. "Honestly?" she asks, and I nod. "No, not really."

My eyes sting at the brutality of those words. But I can't blame her for giving me what I had asked for. I blink away the threatening tears. Now is not the time for breaking down. I have to stay composed.

For a beat, she watches me then continues. "Do you know about Brannigan Enterprises? Hunter didn't form that company all by himself. He and Grayson built it together."

I nod. "I didn't at first, but I know that now."

"Xander?" she asks.

"Yeah."

"What else did he say?"

"Not much," I say, shrugging my shoulders. "Just that Hunter screwed him over and took over the company."

Brielle laughs wryly. "Of course he did."

"Is it not true?" I ask.

She shakes her head slightly. "Well, it's not *not* true. It's just not the whole truth. But that doesn't really matter anyway. The point is Grayson wanted revenge."

"But what does that have to do with you and Hunter having an affair?"

"It has everything to do with it," she says. "You see, our business, Whitmore and Associates, it's been sinking for a while. We made a few poor business decisions, one after the other, and well, we needed an influx of capital or else we'd be headed for receivership."

"I don't understand what that means," I whisper, feeling like a fool.

She sighs. "It means we needed money, or we'd lose the business."

"Oh," I say.

"Look, Marlys," she starts. "The whole thing was business. I slept with him so we had some leverage to coax some cash out of Hunter."

"You mean like blackmail?" I say, leaning forward.

"Such a dirty word. But, yes."

"Is that why things were weird at the dinner party?"

"No, you see. I don't know how he did it, but Hunter

discovered what we were doing. Then he turned the tables and blackmailed us into selling the business."

"Oh my God, really?"

"Yes, really. The deal was that if we sold him the company, he would invest the money we needed to save the business."

"So, you and Grayson would be unemployed and have lost your business as well?" I ask, finally understanding.

"No, actually part of the deal was that we would both keep our jobs, but Hunter would be CEO. We would answer to him directly. He didn't trust us running it ourselves after the string of decisions that led to that point."

"And Grayson just went along with that? After what happened before?"

"He didn't want to, but we were out of options."

I consider all of these new revelations. Maybe Brielle didn't kill Hunter, after all. But given the horrible deal Hunter was forcing, Grayson' motive seems stronger than ever.

"So, what you're saying is, Hunter forced you and Grayson to sell him the company, and you just... accepted it?"

Her lips press together, then exhales slowly. "What choice did we have, Marlys? He had us backed into a corner. If we didn't sell, he was going to destroy us. He had proof— emails, texts, even photos. I don't know how he got them, but he did. And if we went down for extortion, well, in this business, there's no coming back from that. Not ever."

"And Grayson didn't fight it. He just agreed?"

"Not at first. He said he'd rather burn the company to the ground than hand over another business he'd put everything he had into, to Hunter."

"He changed his mind, though?"

Brielle hesitates for a moment. "He knew there was nothing else we could do. Hunter didn't bluff, that wasn't his style. He had enough money to splash around, we both knew he'd happily go there, given the chance. The deal– keeping our jobs, having Hunter tell us how to run our business–it would've been absolutely humiliating, but it was still better than losing everything we worked for."

"Better for you," I mutter under my breath. "What about Grayson? You didn't feel guilty for putting him through that a second time? What if he killed Hunter to save face. Who could blame him given everything you've said?"

Her jaw tightens. "Grayson would never."

"Would never, what?"

She shakes her head. "Nothing. It doesn't matter."

"It does," I insist. "Because if he was angry enough to want revenge, then maybe he's capable of..."

"I told you," Brielle snaps, raising her voice. "Grayson did not kill Hunter."

I frown. "How do you know that?"

"Because he was with me, alright?" she huffs.

I tilt my head, watching her squirm, uncomfortable now that she's shared more than intended. "I thought you said he dropped you home and he went to his house?"

His jaw tightens. "I lied, Okay?"

"Why?"

"My reputation, of course. Look, I have to get back to work now..." Her words trail off, but there's nothing left to squeeze out of her.

I stand. "And... thank you for telling me the truth."

"You're welcome," she says thick with sarcasm, followed by an involuntary snort. "Oh, and Marlys," she says just as I reach the door. "Don't repeat any of this to anyone."

"Why not?"

"Because you're the one they're after."

"Who? The police?" I ask.

Brielle smirks. "Sure. Let's go with that." And just like that, her false demeanour resurfaces, snapping back into place—pristine, calculated, and impenetrable. Like she didn't just admit to destroying my marriage for a flimsy business deal. That she didn't just reveal her blackmail scheme, or that Hunter had cornered her just as tightly as I feel now.

I leave. There's nothing left to say. Not to her.

All the new information whirls about in my head as I walk back to my car, paying no mind to people passing by. I go through the motions—opening the door and sliding into the seat. Seatbelt on, indicator on, side check done, then I pull out onto the road. Ensuring I'm in the lines, my gaze shifts, checking the rear vision mirror. I readjust it into position.

My heart hammers in my chest.

The SUV. It's back. Again.

I grip the steering wheel tighter and press down on the accelerator. The engine revs so hard, for a second, I worry the engine might fall right out of the car. I glance back at the shining black vehicle trailing close behind. So close, if I were to brake right now, they'd smash right into me.

I yank the wheel, pulling the car into the next lane, so quick I don't indicate. It's still there. With another swift move, I shift back into the other lane. And sure enough, they're right there.

Even as my pulse rises, growing faster and more furious, my anger that's been dormant, reignites.

These people, or person, are erratic and maybe even dangerous. But I surprised myself back there at Whitmore and Associates, facing off with Brielle. It was as if an entirely different person, one hidden deep within my subconscious, had emerged today. If I can do it once, I can find the strength to do it again.

Eyes locked on the road, I drive with purpose. Ready and waiting, biding my time.

A strange sense of calm falls over me, and my shoulders relax, now that I've made my decision.

Let them follow.

This ends once and for all.

24

PUSHED TO THE EDGE
KAGE

I wipe my orange-stained fingers against my pants and leave the empty chip packet on the coffee table. Xander tips his head towards it—his silent way of telling me to pick up my shit. Rolling my eyes, I drag myself off the couch and toss it in the bin.

"Wash your hands," he calls after me. I do, but only because my fingers feel gross.

A moment later, I'm back on the couch. Xander's been helping me prepare for my interview with the police. They should've been here by now, and now the bag of cheese balls is churning in my belly. I feel sick about this whole thing, but maybe that's a good thing. If it gets too much, I could throw up on them just to finish early.

It's a nice thought, but I don't think cops care too much about their suspects. Other than trying to pin them for shit, they didn't do. I mean, I've watched plenty of stuff on TV—I know how these things go.

It could be worse. If I identified as a minority, I'd be stressing already. Then again, I'm an orphan now, so maybe they've already tarred me with their agenda. They did it to Marlys, so why not me, too?

I slouch back on the couch and let out a long sigh.

"It'll be fine. I'll be right there with you. Just be honest," he says, narrowing his gaze like he's trying to transmit subliminal thoughts into my head. "But remember, whatever you say, they're going to delve deeper."

"Shit, Xander," I say. "That doesn't help. You're just making me more nervous."

"Well, there's a lot at stake here." He takes a deep breath and lets it out slowly. "Whatever they ask you, just consider your answer carefully before you speak it out loud. Once it's out there, there's no taking it back."

I nod. Normally I hate being lectured to about 'thinking before speaking'. God knows I've heard that more times than I care to remember. But it's not just me I have to think about here. Not that I give a shit about Marlys, or what happens to her. I do care about what happens to me. If they pin Dad's murder on her and lock her up, what does that mean for me? Living on the streets or packing me up and sending me to some family member I barely even know.

Fuck that.

Besides, Marlys doesn't even know how to stand up for herself. She sure as shit couldn't manage to plan a gruesome murder.

The cops arrive, and Xander greets them at the door before bringing them into the room. He sits beside me and gives a quick pat on my shoulder. I know he's trying to be supportive, but it doesn't help. Not even a little bit. Both detectives sit at the other end of the couch, pulling out notebooks and pens.

"Thanks for talking to us today, Kage," Pike says. "I

know it can be a bit daunting, but it won't take too long. We just need to go over a few things to tie up the investigation."

I nod. But it doesn't take a rocket scientist to notice they said 'tie up' the investigation. Does it mean they've found the killer? I glance at Xander. His jaw is tight, controlled, saying nothing. Maybe he didn't notice.

"How are you holding up with everything that's been happening?" Kaur asks.

I shrug. "I'm fine, I guess."

She tilts her head. "I guess it still feels like a dream—or nightmare. Maybe once the funeral is over, it'll feel more real."

"Maybe," I say, though my insides protest her assumption. I'm not some five-year old who can't tell the difference between real and made up. Does she also think I believe in Santa Claus and happy endings, too? Sheesh. Dad's dead. That's about as real as it gets.

Pike clears his throat. "I'm sure it's been a difficult time for everyone. Your father's death was sudden and unexpected. And from what we understand, your relationship with him was strained."

"Yeah? And?" I blurt. Xander side eyes me and gives me a little nudge, like I'm being rude or something, but I don't think the cop's notice. I frown back at him, then turn back to the cops. "Isn't that normal?"

The detective chuckles under his breath, then straightens out his expression again. "You tell me."

"You obviously know we didn't get along. Why else would you be asking me that?" I pause before continuing. "He wasn't exactly father of the year."

"Why don't you tell us in your own words then, Kage?"

"There's not much to tell, honestly. I was a huge

disappointment to him. He loved to tell me that. I tried to avoid him, but that's not difficult when we were the last thing on his priority list."

I recall his angry words. Nothing I did was ever good enough for him. Not my grades, not my sports achievements, nothing. But it doesn't matter now. He's gone, and I stopped caring a long time ago.

Kaur jots something down in her notebook. Probably how much I resent my dad or that I have some sort of unresolved grief. As if that's new information to anyone.

She glances up at me. "Did you and your father ever get physical?"

"No, never got the chance to," I say matter-of-fact.

Kaur's brows furrow. "What do you mean by that, Kage?"

"It means he was never around long enough to do anything, and even if he was, I doubt he'd have the guts." My nose scrunches up involuntarily at the thought.

Beside me, Xander shuffles, then pats between my shoulders. A long quiet moment passes, both cops focussed on their notes.

Pike looks back up, crossing his legs. "Let's talk about the night he went missing. You were home that evening?"

"Yeah."

"And can anyone confirm that?"

"I was in my room, gaming," I say. "Check my Xbox history if you don't believe me."

"So, that's a no, then?"

"Check it," I say, pointing upstairs to my room.

"Oh, we will, but that doesn't account for the entire night, does it?" I frown at him, not knowing what to say to that. "What about Marlys? Did you speak to her at any stage?"

I shrug. "Maybe in the afternoon, before the guests or dad arrived. You'll have to ask her."

"And you didn't attend the dinner party?"

I shake my head. "I never went to those, ever."

"May I ask why not?" Kaur asks, interrupting.

I raise a single eye brow. "Because they're boring as hell. And, Dad wouldn't want me there anyway."

"Kage, do you recall the last time you saw your father?" she continues.

"I don't know, maybe the day before. Thursday. At breakfast, I think."

"So, you didn't see him at all on Friday?"

I shake my head. "Nope."

"Ok, well did you hear him come home, or leave at any time on Friday night? Maybe when he went over to Xander's house." She shoots a quick glance at him, beside me, and I feel him stiffen, though he stays silent.

"No, I had earphones on. Like I said before, I was gaming... all night."

She writes something in her note pad then exchanges words with Pike, but it's too low, almost a whisper, for me to hear. Pike clears his throat again.

"We'd like to ask you a few words about Marlys."

"We don't really talk, so I'm not sure how much help I can be—but go ahead."

Xander's arm wraps around my shoulders, hand resting on top of my arm. He squeezes it and I flinch a little at the pain. I can't believe he did that, and as much as I want to question him about it, his words from earlier flash in my mind.

Think before you speak, Kage.

"Did your dad and Marlys ever fight?" Pike asks.

I glance at Xander, then back at them. "Not that I knew

of." It's true though. Marlys is way too timid to say shit to my dad, and if she ever did try and stand up for herself, I never saw it.

"You never heard them argue?"

I shake my head again. "No, never." I want to say I heard him yell at her a bunch of times, along with all the times he yelled at me. But less is more right now.

A prickle of unseen—ghostly—eyes crawls across my skin. A shiver runs down my spine and shakes my shoulders. I side eye Xander. I know he's watching. But it's more than that. I can feel it, pulse rising higher the more I try to focus.

The hair on one arm rises, goose pimples joining in. But only on my forearm. As if something I can't see is touching me right now.

Then I hear it. So faint, I almost missed it. A shushing sound in my ear. Not the ear adjacent to Xander though, the other side, where it's just the vacant seat.

Liquorice scuttles down the corridor towards the lounge room, bouncing off furniture until she's on the coffee table.

I reach out to pet her, but she pulls away, staring at nothing in the seat beside me. Her back arcs and a thin line of hairs stand straight, trailing down her spine to her upturned tail. Her mouth pulls back, revealing a mouthful of razor-sharp teeth, before a sharp hissing sound emits.

"Liquorice, what's gotten into you?" I say, trying to pet her again. But she just backs up, hissing turns into a growl, hair bristling even more so. Standing, I bend down to pick her up, to calm her. She hesitates, looking past me, then turns and bolts to the stairs. In three swift seconds, her black haze disappears, visible through the bannisters, to the next level of the house.

With a frown, I return to my seat, though Xander's eyes remain firmly set on me. So do the cops.

"Your cat's a little skittish, huh?" Kaur says.

"I guess she's not used to so many people." But in the back of my mind, I know something strange happened just now. I heard someone whisper in my ear, I know that much, but it wasn't Xander. Marlys had told him she thought there was a ghost, but that's ridiculous. He'd said as much, too. But now I'm not so sure. What else could cause Liquorice to behave so wildly?

"Let's circle back to Marlys for a second," she says.

I nod, waiting to see what else they've conjured up.

Pike speaks up. "You said you two don't talk much. Why is that?"

I shift in my seat a little, but Xander grabs me, reassuring me. Why does it matter whether Marlys and I talk,? She's my stepmother, and we all know the story of Cinderella. "I don't know," I shrug. "Don't have much in common."

"Right, but she's been in your life—what—two years now?"

"More like one and a half."

Pike nods, then jots something down. "She hasn't ever tried to connect with you?"

"I guess, but... she can't replace my actual mum, ya know?"

Xander pulls me close and rubs an arm along mine. He turns his head slightly, glancing down at me. "I don't think she's trying to be your mum. She just wants to love you, Kage."

I roll my eyes. I don't want to hear it right now. Biting my tongue, I resist the urge to call him out on that bullshit.

"Xander, you're obviously very close to both Marlys and

Kage. Perhaps you can shed some light on their relationship," Kaur says. They watch him expectantly.

Shifting in his seat, Xander crosses an ankle over one knee, and leans back. "Both Marlys and Kage mean a lot to me. They've been through enough."

"That's not what I asked," Pike says, tipping his head forward, his dark eyes dart between Xander and me, like he's trying to read between the lines.

He takes in a long breath, then lets it out with a whoosh. "It's not my place to judge either of them. I've never been married myself, or had children, so it wouldn't be right for me to do that."

"I see. Well, perhaps you can tell us what you have seen—objectively speaking."

He hesitates and looks at me as if he's seeking my approval.

"Go ahead. I don't care what you say." The more time they take speaking with him, the less I have to. And, it also means, I can take a short break from finding the right words to make them all happy.

"Alright then," he says, patting my leg like I'm a 'good boy' or something. Woof fucking woof to that. "I know Marlys has tried hard to fit into the family, to love both Hunter and Kage. But she's struggled. I mean, I can imagine it's one thing to love another if it's reciprocated, but loving someone who is constantly at odds with you—that's another challenge entirely. Not that it stopped her. It didn't, and it hasn't. She's forever thinking up new ways to..." Xander glances at me. "To bridge the gap, so to speak. And well, Kage... He's strong, and resilient, but he's had a lot of ups and downs in his life, with his mother leaving when he was so young. But because of that, he's got some serious walls up. Too defensive for his own good."

I frown at Xander. How dare he say that shit? My mother is no one's business but my own, and she's definitely not any part of this story. My pulse rises angrily, daring the two authoritative figures at the end of the couch to say something that will give me reason to outwardly object.

He must notice my mood and raises a hand, rubbing it in circles on my upper back. "Kage, I'm sorry that upsets you, but it is the truth. No one is saying that's a bad thing."

"Whatever," I say, rolling my eyes.

"I'm sensing some tension between you two," Kaur says. "Kage, do you often feel angry?"

"No," I snap. As soon as the word has left my mouth, I realise my error. Both cops are staring at me, brows raised. "I mean, no. I'm angry now, because you're asking all this personal stuff that's none of your business, but I'm not always that way."

Pike raises a finger and thumb to his chin, and rubs it like he's trying to work out how much truth there is in my words. Something flickers in his eyes, like he's celebrating their win at knocking me from my comfort zone. "Is that something you get from your father? Being quick to anger?"

My eyes widen involuntarily. "I'm nothing like him. Don't you dare..."

"Kage, that's enough," Xander interjects, flashing me a look that says 'shut the hell up before you get yourself into hotter water'.

A heaviness settles in my chest. Lowering my voice, I practically plead with him. "You don't really think that, Xander, do you? I'm not like him, I promise." I shake my head.

He shifts around to face me fully, and grabs me by both shoulders, almost shaking me. "No, Kage. No one who knows you, thinks that. I promise you." He stays like that for a few seconds while I take in his words, then his hands fall, turning back to the cops.

"Are you done here?"

"Almost. I just have two more questions," Pike says.

"Then let's wrap it up," Xander urges them, hugging an arm around my shoulder.

"Right, Kage, judging from what we've seen and heard today, there's no love lost between you and your dad. Perhaps you're even a bit relieved that he's out of your life now. And maybe that hate motivated you to commit murder."

What the actual fuck!

Words scramble in my head, jumbled, mixing with the fury now raging in my veins. I want to scream at them, to tell them they don't know what the fuck they're talking about. That my dad—*Hunter*—had it coming. He treated everyone like a piece of shit. They all had 'motive', more than any 'anger' I ever felt. And to single me out now, suggesting I'm the culprit... it's too much.

All I can do is shake my head, and a tiny voice in my ear says to speak up, to tell them. "It wasn't me, I swear."

"Last question," Xander says in a gruff, no nonsense tone.

Pike nods. "If you didn't kill him, did Marlys?"

One second they're accusing me, the next they're accusing Marlys. Who's next? Xander. What a joke. They're just grasping at straws. And to think I let them get under my skin like that. I've never felt more foolish in my life.

"Marlys?" I say, scrunching my nose up at them. "She couldn't hurt a fly, even if she tried." I shake my head. "You're definitely barking up the wrong tree. Maybe try looking at his business dealings instead."

"Is there something you know about Brannigan Enterprises that you're not telling us?"

"I'm just saying, if I were you, I'd spend less time interrogating innocent family members, and look at someone else with an actual motive—like that gold digging bitch my dad had an affair with. It's a no-brainer."

An awkward silence fills the room for a long moment. I've said enough—probably too much. But now it's time to stop.

Pike stands. "You seem pretty convinced about that. What are you basing that on?"

I cross my arms. "You think Marlys, or I are capable of murder, but you don't think the woman who was sleeping with my dad, and who just so happens to be drowning in financial ruin, would have a reason to off him?"

He scribbles something in his notebook.

Good. Write that shit down.

Now go and investigate it, like it's your *job*.

Kaur pipes up. "You truly believe that Brielle Maddox had a motive?"

I snort. "Oh, I know she did."

Xander's hand grips my shoulder, firmer than before. I glance at him and frown. Though something in his eyes, unsure whether it's a beg or a threat, says to quiet.

I say a silent prayer. Please don't ask me how I know. Please.

"Right, I think that's everything for now," Pike says, and heads towards the front door.

And just like that, like a snap of the fingers, we're done. It feels like a trick, but then the other detective follows him out as well. Xander speaks low, ushering them out. I hover behind him, watching them go back to their car.

Moments later, the car disappears into the suburbs.

Xander begins to close the door, when Marlys pulls up into the driveway. Then another car pulls up behind her, blocking her in. It's a large, dark SUV, with windows so black it practically reflects the sun.

Marlys jumps out of the car.

"What the fuck?" Xander says. "Is that the car that's been following her?"

"The what?" I say. This is all news to me. I stand there, unsure of what is going on right now, though it seems Xander and Marlys have been hiding something.

"The notes, the SUV, they're connected." The words rush out of his mouth without a second thought. "Just stay here, don't do anything."

At the same time, Marlys storms over to the SUV. Her fists are balled up, and she raises one to the car's window. The bang is loud, and it's a surprise it doesn't shatter with the force. The car sits there, unmoving. She raises a foot to the door, ballet flat shoe flying off in her haste. A louder bang, dinting the perfect paint of the car's exterior.

"What the fuck is she doing?" I say to Xander, who's equally confused. "It's like she's possessed or something. I've never seen her like this before."

The Marlys I know would apologise to a damn mannequin if she bumped into it. Now she's out here, battering someone's car like a freaking lunatic.

Marlys screams something at the driver, but her voice is so furious the words all blur together. The door cracks open. She quietens and steps back, but she remains focused, ready. A person shifts through the gap, and Xander takes a step down the stairs, then another, until he's halfway to her.

A tall, slender man in a hoodie steps out onto the footpath, closing the door behind him—they're talking—but I can't hear anything. I dart out of the house, trailing behind

Xander—whether to be at the ready for Marlys, or to make sure I see the drama unfold personally, I don't know. And it doesn't matter right now.

A slow, eerie smirk creeps across the man's face, then in a voice so calm it's terrifying he speaks. "You kept her from me. Now we fix that."

25

SPINNING

MARLYS

My heart hammers in my chest, fuelled by the rage that courses through my veins. I don't think there's ever been a time in my life where I've felt more in control of my actions, but also completely out of control. It's weird and strange, like my body has been disconnected from my brain and taken over by something else entirely.

I know it's a response from repressing my thoughts and feelings for so long. From refusing to deal with my baggage. My trauma. From being pushed down, shoved around, and emotionally left for dead.

Now every calm and rational thought has left me in the wake of impulse and fury. I'm done feeling hunted, and at the mercy of whomever is behind those notes, the SUV, and every whisper of dread that followed me since Hunter disappeared.

My ballet flat skids against the pavement as I storm toward the black SUV. Hands balled into fist so tight my nails dig into my palms. But the pain only reminds me of the emotional turmoil I've been dragged through, like a washing machine constantly set on spin. Round and round it goes, spinning me wildly, until every ounce of energy and reason has been wrung out.

The blacked-out windows are soulless, just like the person hiding inside. They think they can evade me. Not this time. I'm not playing anymore.

I slam my fist against the window. "Get out," I scream, my voice is savage and raw, fuelled by my ire.

There's no movement. No sound. Nothing.

Again, I bang my fist—harder this time. "Get the fuck out." A pang, scratchy and sore, in my throat forces out a cough. Then another. Until finally my throat clears.

Still nothing.

Renewed energy fills me, adrenaline no doubt. It spreads through my veins like wildfire, burning as it races throughout my body. If I have to I'll wage war on this person today.

I kick at the door. The ballet flat flies off my foot, rendering it naked as it impacts against the metal. Pain travels from my toes to my ankle and up my leg, though the satisfaction of leaving my mark cushions the blow.

The door creaks open ever so slightly, gaze unwavering, until I hear my name.

"Marlys, what the hell are you doing?" Xander calls out. His panicked voice, unable to stop me. I spin back to face the car.

A tracksuit covered leg appears first, then an arm, followed by a hoodie covered head. I take a slow step backwards, clenching my fists, ready for whatever comes next. Even if I lose.

The man steps outside, shoving the door closed behind. I strain to see if anyone else is in there, but it's occluded from my gaze too quickly. He raises his head, and using both hands, slides back the hoodie.

He stands there, a sly smirk nagging at the corner of his mouth. Everything in me screams to slap it right off his face, yet something is holding me back, like an invisible string, tied to my hands and waist.

It's him. The man from the care home. The one who came at me like a feral dog. The one I barely escaped. I should've known it was him, and I should've expected this.

His gaze flicks from me to Xander behind me, then to Kage, who's followed him over. Then it returns to me. His eyes practically burn through mine, his anger growing at the same rate as mine.

"What the hell do you want from me?" I spit out the words.

His smirk curls, growing wider, like something you might see in a slasher film, right before the perp pulls out the blood-soaked butcher knife.

"You kept her from me. Now we fix that," he says, voice low and rough.

A gush of cold, biting wind whips around the front lawn. It sends goose pimples over my skin, and I shiver. It spurs me and I shift forward, but that invisible pull tugs me back. Xander steps forward, placing himself between me and the man.

"You need to leave. Now."

"Not until you let me see her." He narrows his eyes at Xander.

"Who?" I interject through their tension.

"Don't play dumb, Marlys. You recognise me. You visited *her*.

Words choke in my throat. I swallow hard, trying to clear it. He's talking about Amelia.

"Did you kill Hunter to get to Amelia?" I ask.

The man takes a step forward, now standing over me. He's at least a foot taller than I am. A palpable tension, almost like electricity, zaps between us. His intimidation is obvious, but I refuse to back down. I step on tiptoes, trying to meet his gaze. To make it clear I'm not scared. Though my insides are reeling, waiting for him to grab me and hurt me. I know Xander won't allow that.

"I asked you a question," I growl at him.

His dark eyes shift closer, challenging me with a cold stare. Everything in me says to flee, but I hold firm. My eyes are grainy and dry, but I force them open. I'm not giving in.

His nostrils flare, and a low rumble slides out of my mouth.

Xander places one hand on the guy's shoulder.

"Settle down. You don't want to hit a woman, do you?"

Xander's words hit him hard and the man falters. "Get your hand off me."

Xander lifts both hands, taking a step back, and the guy does the same.

"Look," I say, trying to intervene. I glance around the street: neighbours hover at their fence lines, pretending to water their gardens but their eyes are firmly fixed on my front lawn. "I'm not keeping her from you. I didn't even know who she was until the other day."

The man watches me, like he's trying to figure out if I'm being honest.

"I don't know why, but Hunter put her there. He kept her a secret from me, too. I'm trying to piece this all together myself."

"Bullshit," he says, then runs a hand through his short brown hair.

"Whether you believe me or not, that's on you. But I'm

telling you, I had nothing to do with it." I pause for a minute. He avoided answering my question, that still burns in the back of my mind. I lower my voice. "You wrote those notes, didn't you?"

He laughs, but it quivers with nervous energy. It's as good as a confession in my book. "You want answers? Well, so do I."

I fold my arms, standing taller. "Then start speaking."

He sucks in a deep breath, exhaling slowly before meeting my gaze again. "I didn't kill Hunter. I had nothing to do with that. Although, the thought crossed my mind plenty of times." He rubs the back of his neck.

My eyebrows raise high on my forehead. That's a pretty brazen thing to admit, though if he was the killer, I doubt he'd have admitted that to me. "Then why have you been stalking me?"

"Stalking?" He shakes his head and a bitter laugh follows. "I was trying to get your attention. To get you to tell me the truth."

"And you thought that was the best way to do it?" Xander interjects. "Geez."

I place a hand on Xander's forearm, and flash a look, telling him to let me do this myself. "I told you I didn't know about her, not 'til I saw her for myself."

"And I found out about Hunter the same way everyone else did—on TV," he says. Studying him, I realise he's either a damn good actor, or he's telling the truth. "Now, can I see my sister, please?"

I frown and shake my head. "You don't even know if she wants to see you."

"She's my sister. Doesn't that count for something?"

"Maybe, but don't you think she deserves a say in this as well?"

"So, what then?" he asks.

"Perhaps Marlys can visit her again, and talk it through," Xander suggests.

"I can do that," I nod.

"Fine," he huffs. "But don't drag this out. She's been through enough for too long already."

He jumps back into the drivers seat, and is out of sight in moments. Though I still feel a little uneasy.

"That guy is unhinged," Xander says, wrapping his arms around me. I bury my face into his chest, finally able to breathe. "You okay?"

"Yeah, I'm fine," I mumble into his shirt. He rubs my back and finally my pulse quiets. I pull back. "I guess I'll be doing another road trip then."

"Do you want me to come?" he offers.

"No, it's fine.".

"I'd like to go," Kage speaks up. I'd completely forgotten he was out here. Warmth rushes up my neck, spreading to my face, embarrassed that he just witnessed me losing all control like that.

"Sorry, Kage," I say. "You shouldn't have seen that."

He chuckles. "I'm glad I saw it. You were so... different. Badass, actually."

My heart swells at his words, and I choke back tears. Apparently, all it took to close the gap between us—for him to see me as a person—was to lose my mind. Who knew?

I smile at him. "Uh, thanks Kage."

"One more thing," he says. "I want to see Amelia. I don't really remember her, but she was my step-mum, too."

"I don't know..." I start, but he cuts me off.

"Please... I'll owe you."

"Alright, we'll go tomorrow," I say.

"Sweet, thanks, Marlys."

Xander and I remain on the front lawn, oblivious to the neighbours still hovering about, as Kage heads back inside. Probably for more gaming, though in this moment, none of that bothers me.

"Xander," I say, low so no one else hears. "Do you believe he had nothing to do with Hunter's death?"

He shrugs. "I can't be certain, but I don't think so."

Xander shifts to stand in front of me, so close that I can feel his breath on my lips. His voice is gravelly and low as he speaks. "But one thing I know for sure—you're safe with me. You and Kage."

Then his lips are on mine. Soft, warm, and reassuring.

I sink into it, letting him pull me in, letting me believe it. His arms tighten around my waist, pressing me flush against his chest, his heart pounding just as fast as mine.

It's everything I'd daydreamed it would be. Everything I've needed.

Everything I once thought I had before.

The thought penetrates through the warmth—my relationship with Hunter started with a kiss just like this. That same comforting embrace, that same promise of protection.

And look how that turned out.

I squeeze my eyes shut, willing the thought away. Xander isn't Hunter. He's nothing like him. He always knows exactly what I need. What to say to pull me back from the edge. I can trust him.

The ache in my chest tightens, but Xander deepens the kiss, and I let him.

I can't think about that now. To let old doubts resurface. Not when I finally feel safe.

26

———————

THREE MOTHERS

MARLYS

The weight of Hunter's past deeds sits heavy in my chest. And although my head says it's not my responsibility to amend, my heart says otherwise. There's probably a thousand more secrets still buried, but the deed most pressing, that needs resolving, is Amelia.

She deserved better.

Better than a half-present husband. Better than the shell of a life she's been trapped in since he locked her away.

But that's not all he took.

He stole her future. Her choices. I know her family loves her, and her brother went through hell just to find her again. But it wasn't just that. She could've done so much—achieved so much more, in the decade since she's been here. Perhaps she'd have met a kind, loving man. One who would cherish her. And maybe she'd have had children—her own, or others from a blended family. Or a career. So many lost opportunities. Who's to say what could have been?

The world still holds so much more for her, the future

and all that's meant to be. Her destiny, put on ice, now hers to reclaim.

And I hope she finds it.

All of it.

All the love, the hope, the joy, the laughter—the smallest things that drive us on, to get up each morning, to strive through the hardships, just to find a humble seed of that which makes life great.

I want that for Kage, too.

And, if I let myself believe it, maybe even for me.

I tap my finger against the steering wheel and glance over at Kage in the front passenger seat. "Almost there. Are you nervous?"

He shrugs. "Not really." He turns and looks out the window, then adds. "Maybe a little bit."

I expected as much. He hasn't seen her since he was little. It's not surprising he couldn't recall her sooner. From what I knew, after his mother left, Hunter had hired help to care for his son. For a child, it must have been so confusing. Women coming and going from his life like that. That's why I've tried so hard to be there for him, even when he shut me out at every turn.

I reach over and lay a hand on his forearm. "It's alright if you've changed your mind."

His head snaps back to face me. "No, I want to see her."

"Okay, then," I pat his arm before returning my hand to the wheel, pulling into the car park.

Weaving through parked cars, I glance at Kage. His hands are deep in his pockets, shoulders stiff. I close the gap between us, loosely wrapping an arm around his shoulder in an effort to reassure him. It's something I've never done before and hope it's not a faux pas. He stops and turns to face me, brows furrowed.

I grimace and withdraw my arm. "Too much?"

"Yeah."

Once we're inside, I move ahead to the reception area while Kage looks around.

Recognising the woman from my last visit, I force a sweet smile. "Hi."

"Good morning," she replies. "Are you here to see Amelia again?"

"Uh, yeah," I say. "You remembered?"

She nods curtly. "Yes, I remember everyone." She taps a finger at her temple and raises an eyebrow.

"I brought someone with me," I say. "Kage," I call out to him, who's still hovering a few metres away, checking out the place. I wave, beckoning for him to join me. He drags his feet, ambling slowly to the desk. "This is my stepson, Kage."

The woman tips her head. "Nice to meet you, Kage." He grunts out something symbolising a hello. She turns to the computer and taps on the keyboard. "There's still the matter of the power of attorney and the visitor list." She taps some more. "Oh," her voice drops low. "I'm very sorry for your loss, Mrs Brannigan, and Kage."

"Actually, that's why we're here. I need to discuss what Amelia would like to do, since Hunter... um, isn't her power of attorney anymore."

"Yes, I can see there's a notation from your solicitor here. You're fine to see her, but please update us as soon as it's all worked out. We need to keep it on the up and up."

"Of course, just as soon as I figure it out."

"Right, well, you remember the way?" She gestures towards the doors leading to the residential wings.

"Yeah, we've got it," I say, hitching my bag's strap over my shoulder. "Thanks."

We follow the corridors to Harmony East wing, then

down to Amelia's room. I stop just before we get there, turning to face Kage straight on.

I place a gentle hand on his shoulder. "Ready?"

"Yep."

"Okay, then," I say, stealing my hand back.

Amelia's bedroom door is ajar. I raise my hand, tapping a happy tune with my knuckles. I want to keep this meeting upbeat for Kage.

"Come in," Amelia says from inside the room.

Pushing the door open wider, I shuffle inside, Kage following behind. Amelia is resting on top of her bed, holding a thick novel. Though by the looks of the pink leggings and Lycra crop top she's wearing, she must've been doing yoga earlier.

She swings her legs around into a sitting position on the edge of the bed. "Marlys?" she says. "I was wondering when I'd see you again." Her gaze shifts behind me, and her neck stretches. "Who's with you?"

I turn to Kage and place one hand behind him, guiding him forward. "Amelia, you remember Kage?"

Her eyes widen, mouth dropping. She stares for a long moment, then smiles. "Kage, oh my goodness. You've grown so much." She shakes her head. "I can't believe it's been so long." Amelia pats the bed beside her. "Come sit."

Kage hesitates for a moment, glancing at me like he's looking for permission. And I relish the feeling. It's a first for us. Almost like respect. I nod, letting the relief and joy within spread to my face as I watch the two of them exchange small talk.

"I don't really remember much," he says, head hanging low, staring at the floor. "Dad got rid of all your photos and stuff." He raises his head, turning to face her. "But I remember little things," he pauses. "And sometimes I see your face in my dreams."

"Oh, sweetheart," Amelia says, placing her hand on his. "It's alright. My memory is a little patchy too, but I can remember enough for the both of us."

She asks him about school, and what hobbies he's into. And as Amelia shares little snippets of their time together, when Kage was younger, I realise this is the closure that both of them needed.

I slide into a chair by the window, leaning an elbow on the armrest, my head in my hand. Even as an outsider to this reunion, the joy is spread amongst us. It's a rare gem given the past few weeks, but I know I'll have to brace the truth of our visit soon.

Amelia notices me. "I'm so sorry, Marlys. We're being rude."

I wave a hand, truly not concerned. "No, it's fine. I'm just glad for this moment."

A broad smile spreads over her face, and her eyes sparkle in the morning light filtering through the window. "How have you been?" she says.

I sigh. "I'm a little rough around the edges, but I'm okay."

Her smile falters. "I heard about Hunter." Her eyes darken like she's wary of bringing him up. "What happened?"

It's interesting that she's the first person since Hunter's death that hasn't shared her condolences. And perhaps there's a reason for that.

I shake my head. "The police are still investigating." I consider sharing everything that's come to light, but she's already been through one ordeal with him. I don't see the point in hurting her further.

She nods, as if reading between the lines, then clears her throat. "And the funeral? When will that be?"

I glance at Kage, minding my words. "We're still waiting to hear. He's with the coroner." I pause. "Once they've given me a final report, they'll let us know so we can plan something." Another hesitation. "Would you like to attend?"

Amelia raises a hand to the back of her head, then lowers it again. "Maybe."

Pushing her will do no good. This has to be her choice.

Despite the comfortable temperature in the room, she shivers. Her gaze flickers towards the open bedroom door. Her eyes narrow, and something shifts in her expression, focussing on something I can't see. Just as quickly as she looked, she snaps out of it, returning her attention to me and forcing a smile.

"So, did you two just come to reminisce, or is there something you want to talk about?"

I nod and shift in my chair. "Actually, I wanted to speak to you about your brother."

Her brows pull together. "My brother? James?"

James. I hadn't even thought to ask him his name before now. Yet, I'm grateful for the information.

"Yes," I say, keeping my tone even. "The thing is, Hunter was your power of attorney, and now he's gone we need to figure out... what's next." I watch as she takes in the meaning of my words. "He would like to see you. And take care of you."

"Really?" she beams. "I thought they'd left me to rot in here, too."

I shake my head. "No, that was all Hunter's doing." I lower my voice. "No one knew you were here. None of us did."

Amelia stares at me, processing the jagged truth. I glance between her and Kage, unsure of what to say. He lifts an arm, wrapping it around her, just like I tried to do earlier in the car park. It's all that's needed to pull her attention, and she leans into him.

"If we knew, we would've come to visit," he says. His gaze shoots to me, empathy radiating from him. It's new and different, for him, *my* teenage stepson. Pride swells in my heart, but we both know Hunter would never have allowed us to visit. Amelia knows this too, and soaks up every ounce of love he gives.

"Well, it's your decision, Amelia. I don't want to tell you what to do or how to live your life. But if you want James to take over, if you want to see him, all you have to do is say so."

"You would do that for me?" she says. Her voice is so small, like she is afraid to believe it. "You barely even know me."

"The thing is, Amelia, we're more alike than you know."

She sits up straighter and brushes a stray hair from her face. "How do you mean?"

I tilt my head, smiling weakly. "I know what it's like to have your choice and freedom stripped away. To have someone else control everything you do." I shake my head. "You don't deserve that. You deserve every good thing this world can offer, and not an ounce less." I suck in a deep breath, then exhale slowly. "I know what my husband was. And I know I'm not the first." A tear glistens in her eye, but she just keeps watching me. "Hunter was obsessed with control, but he also knew how to suck you in. He made me feel like the most important person in the world—until he didn't." I shake my head, feeling my own tears prickle. I blink, forcing them back. "By the time I realised how unhappy I was, I was trapped in my own life." I glance at Kage, feeling a little guilty for speaking about his father this way. How he must feel hearing these words about his own flesh and blood. His brow furrows, and his lips draw into a thin line. "I'm sorry, Kage. I tried; I really did. And as much as I wanted to leave, I couldn't go. Not knowing what you'd be left with."

Tears begin to fall, trailing down my cheeks. Through the blur, I see Amelia squeeze Kage's hand.

"You stayed for Kage, *too*," she says flashing a sympathetic smile.

"Too?" Kage speaks up, brows furrowed towards Amelia.

She nods. "Everything Marlys just said, well, I understand it. All of it. But the cards weren't in my favour, or Miranda's, for that matter." She turns to me. "You got lucky,. Be thankful for gracious deeds, no matter how grievous they may seem."

"I don't understand," Kage says, jaw tightening. "You could've just left and taken me with you."

"Well, that's all in the past now," Amelia says, squeezing his hand again. "Now we can all live our lives."

"Easy for you to say," he grumbles under his breath. "You have someone to take care of you. What am I going to do? I have no one."

I can't believe what I'm hearing. Kage believes that I would let him face this world alone. My struggle as a parent have been real, and I've failed at so many things. But this, if he truly believes this of me, well then, I've failed at the most important thing. Letting him know I have his back—always.

I frown. "Kage," I shake my head. "I would never abandon you. Not now, not ever."

He watches me like he doesn't believe a word coming

out of my mouth, but that doesn't make it any less true. But if there's anything I know about Kage, no one can force him to believe or do anything. He can raise it with me when he's ready.

"So," I say to Amelia. "Do you know what you'd like to do?"

She nods and a smile curls at the corner of her lips. "If James really does want to take care of me after all this time, then let him."

"And the power of attorney?"

"Give it to him."

"Okay then. I'll get it sorted as soon as we get home." I take a moment before speaking again. "Any idea what you'll do from here on out?"

Amelia shrugs her shoulders. "Like you said, anything is possible now. But I think I'll just see what each day brings."

"Anyway, we have a bit of a drive home. We'd better get a move on," I say.

Pulling Kage close, she embraces him for a long moment. When she pulls back, she cups his face in her hands, smiling.

"I'm so proud of the man you're becoming, Kage. Don't let your father's shadow follow you. You're so much more than his son."

"Thanks," he says, glancing around like he can't hold her gaze any longer. In case her emotion washes off on him, too.

"You have two mothers now," I say, pointing a finger between myself and Amelia. "We're not going anywhere."

Amelia nods. "Three actually."

It's a curious thing to say, but the moment is so heartfelt, I let it slide. Kage shifts off the bed and shares one last hug before trailing back to the car alongside me.

Neither of us says a word as we climb into the car and leave the care home in our wake. I wonder what's next for Amelia. Whether she'll leave the place she's called home for a decade. But then again, as lovely as it seems, it's also been her prison. She's been given the key. Now all she has to do is plan her escape. Her brother, her accomplice, lighting the fuse that will smash those walls holding her in.

In a way, our home is like that. Isn't it? Reminders of Hunter, everywhere I look. Maybe after the funeral, when the will has been read and actioned, maybe opportunity waits for me too. A fresh start. How would Kage feel about that? Uprooting everything that he's called home his whole life and starting over some place new. Somewhere we can be the people we choose to be, without worrying about the fractures that hold us together. I'd miss Xander though, as would Kage. The way he's supported us through this ordeal is second to none. He stepped up when no one else dared to. Then again, stealing Kage away—and hurting my heart in the process—perhaps that's not the best idea.

I shake my head at the thought and refocus on the road before us. From the corner of my eye, I see Kage watching me. He probably thinks I'm nuts right now, shaking my head for no apparent reason. I doubt its anything he hasn't thought before.

"Marlys," he says, shifting around to face me better. "Can I talk to you about something?"

"Of course. What's on your mind?" I reply, flashing a quick glance, before looking back at the road.

He's fidgeting, staring at his hands. "I've been having these dreams..." His voice trails off like he's trying to work out how to tell me what's going on.

"What sort of dreams? Like nightmares?"

"No, they're just," he sighs. "Weird." The tone in his voice sounds like he's screwing up his face.

"Weird how?" I flash another quick glance his way.

"Don't judge me, Okay?"

I nod but say nothing, giving him the space to find the right words.

"Well, I keep seeing this woman. Her body stays the same, but her face... I don't know, it kind of morphs."

I hum softly, letting him know I'm listening.

"One second, it's my mum, and then—it shifts. Like the eyes change, the mouth, everything. You know what I mean, right?"

I hum again.

"Well, here's the really weird part. I didn't remember Amelia's face until I saw her today. But it's her face that my mum's changes into."

My brows pull together tightly, but I nod, taking it all in.

"That's weird, right?" he says. "What do you think it means?"

I suck in a deep breath, exhaling through my nose. This isn't exactly my wheelhouse, but I have to give him something. But confusion engulfs my mind, too. How can he be seeing two faces if one is his mother, and one is Amelia? Aren't they one and the same?

Unless they aren't.

Maybe his grief is affecting him far worse than I thought. Or maybe, there's something I've overlooked.

27

THE BOX

MARLYS

What had Amelia said, the first time we'd met? Something cryptic about the stairwell? Perhaps it holds a clue to at least one more secret. One more of Hunter's deeds that needs resolution.

I haven't mentioned it to Kage yet, not wanting to get his hopes up. Right now, he's in his room, on Xbox with his friends, no doubt. The time is as good as any, while I'm by myself.

I stare at the small doorway leading to the dead space beneath the stairs. It's more of a hatch really, standing half the height of a regular door, and a little less wide. In another life, it could've been transformed into a child's playhouse, perhaps.

The door sticks a little and I have to jiggle it before it creaks open. Inside, it's dark as night except for the light from the lounge room. Dust motes linger in the musty air. Only the centre is lit; the corners remain dark. Boxes of various sizes occupy the space. Some have handwritten labels, but others remain clueless about their contents.

The first box I grab is easy, standing next to the

doorway. A medium-sized box, a top another large one. I drag both out into the lounge room, setting them on the coffee table. Neither have labels, and I open the smaller one to discover old magazines. Curious, I flip through them: homewares from the early 2000s, finance and investment issues, women's gossip rags, and at the very bottom, explicit magazines. I roll my eyes and set the box aside, opening the larger one to find bed linen. Putting that aside too, I sigh, before heading back to the space.

Next, I grab another three boxes stacked together. Sifting through each one, it's much of the same—more homewares and linens, and some old men's clothes. Someone should have donated this junk to charity instead of hoarding it.

After another half hour, boxes fill the lounge room, scattered about the place, while the tiny room slowly empties. Despite my efforts, I've found nothing resembling what Amelia mentioned. Using my phone's flashlight, I checked what's left.

Just a few boxes. One of them must be it.

I put my phone in my mouth, holding on tightly, and crawl towards the very back. A small cardboard box, unlike the others, and more like a gift box, is pushed all the way into the corner. Something is wrapped around the centre. Sticky tape, perhaps? I reach for it, fingers outspread, trying not to hit my head on the underside of the steps. I shift closer, into a spider web. Shaking my head, the phone falls from my mouth.

I pick it up and try again, finally touching the smooth surface. With fingertips, desperately flick it towards me. After a few failed attempts, it finally budges, sliding over the floorboards. I inch it closer until I can get a proper grasp.

My pulse rises as I pull it towards me. Once in my

hands, I shift, sitting upright cross-legged in the space. The lounge room lights up the floral pattern, and the yellowing, fragile tape wrapped around the middle.

This has to be it. The box Amelia was talking about.

Slowly, I peel back the dry tape. It's no longer sticky, leaving a yellow ring around on the boxes otherwise white background.

Should call Kage down so he can share in whatever is inside? But then again, why get his hopes up? There's no proof this actually has anything to do with his mother. Miranda. Perhaps it belongs to Amelia. Or someone Hunter dated in between.

I run a hand over the top, clearing aside the gathering of dust that was a decade in the making. My fingertips sizzle with an electric buzz, like it's cautioning me. Something pushes me to open it, but I'm not sure whether it's my internal thoughts or something else entirely. But it makes my heart pound faster, urgent.

Delicately, I begin to lift one corner.

A rush of cold whips around me, as if I'm standing on the edge of a cyclone. I close my eyes, trying to stay my racing thoughts. Everything in me is screaming to run, to escape this unnatural... whatever it is. But then I see her face in my mind's eye.

The same women in the photos from Kage's room. And the same voice I thought was in my head. I summon all the courage I can and dare myself to speak.

"Miranda?" I say in a low whisper.

Another rush of frozen air circles me, dropping the temperature ten degrees. I shudder, shoulders shivering involuntarily. Then it disappears like it was never even there. Then an almost indecipherable whisper comes.

"Yes."

The box rocks in my lap as if it wants to be opened. To free whatever is being held inside. My hands tremble but return to the corner that's still sitting ajar. Cautiously, I lift it, wary of anything that might rush out. Geckos, or cockroaches, even mice. Or... something else. The fear is fleeting, as the lid comes off, and I rest it on the floor beside me.

On top sits an envelope, and beneath it a collection of what appears to be varying knickknacks. I pick up the envelope and flip it over. It isn't even sealed. I slip a finger in, pulling out the single page note, and unfold it.

The note begins with, 'Dear Kage.'

I hesitate, staring at his name. It feels like I'm overstepping, as if I'm reading someone's diary. My gaze jumps to the bottom of the page.

'Always in my heart, Your Mother, M.'

My throat tightens, and I hold my breath for just a moment. This isn't just some note, it's from mother to son. And probably the last words she will ever say to him. My stomach sinks, and a pang of sadness flows over me for the loss they've both endured. It's no wonder she still lingers here.

I try to call out to Kage, but my voice catches in my throat. Only a strangled mess of words comes out. I try again, without much improvement. Clearing my throat, I force out the words, louder this time.

"Kage," I yell, leaning out of the doorway, turning my face towards the stairwell. "Come down here." The urgency in my voice is reflective of the situation, and Kage appears at the top of the steps, glancing down over the balustrades.

"You called?" he says.

"Come here, quick."

He flashes a strange glance my way, but races down the

stairs. Kage crouches at the small hatch-like door, peering in.

"What the hell are you doing in there?"

"Here," I say, "You're going to want to sit down for this."

He takes the box I pass through, brows pulling together. "What is it?"

"Amelia mentioned it the first time I visited her." I hesitate. "She said there was something... under the stairwell." I meet his gaze, willing him to understand before I say it out loud. "Kage, I think this box belonged to your mother."

Kage's grip tightens around the edges of the box. Then he takes a slow step backwards. I crawl out, swatting at the dust on my jeans.

He's stares at the box in his hands. I reach out, gently touching his arm.

"Come on. Let's sit," I say, guiding him over to the couch where we settle side by side.

Kage plays with one corner almost like he's daring himself to open it. All I can do is give him time. To process, to remember, to find what little memories he still holds in the back of his mind.

The temperature shifts again, cooler but without the churning breeze from before. She must be waiting, watching. The hope is insufferable, and for the briefest of moments, it's almost as if I'm feeling what she is.

Finally, Kage pries the corner open, carefully lifting the lid off as if it's some sort of ancient antique. I'm sure the box's value is equal in his eyes.

Suddenly, I spot an indent on the couch. On the other side of Kage. Like someone just sat beside him. My gaze shifts from the cushion to the backrest.

I inhale sharply. He turns his head towards the dent,

rubbing his arm where goose pimples erupt. Kage turns to me, saying nothing. But he doesn't have to. His eyes say everything. An unspoken acknowledgment shared between us. I simply nod towards the letter.

He picks it up, retrieving the note, and reads quietly.

I desperately want to read it, but force myself to wait. I can't intrude on. If he wants to share it, he will. Kage leans forward, and places the folded note on the coffee table, on top of it's envelope, then returns to the box.

Kage picks up a pair of baby booties, joined together with a tiny plastic peg. It's baby blue with white edging, with a motif of a baby elephant on the sides. He sets them aside with the note and lifts out a necklace. The tarnished gold reveals a filigree locket. With his fingernail, he unlocks it. Inside are two small pictures—one of a baby, the other a woman. A tiny blonde curl, rests in between, that matches the baby's hair colouring.

Kage digs through several more items, to the bottom where a photograph lays, encased in a silver frame.

My hand flies to my mouth, and I gasp. In the photo, there are two women and a toddler. The child, I assume, is Kage, and the woman I've never seen before must be Miranda. But the second woman I've both seen and spoken with.

Kage's brows pull together, turning to me. "Amelia knew my mum? Why didn't she tell me?" he asks, like I have the answer to his question.

Amelia never mentioned this to me. She acted as if the Miranda she knew was all but a ghost haunting her in this house. The fact she knew her—and was maybe even friends —takes all the breath out of my lungs.

"I don't know, I guess so," is all I can bring myself to reply. But then I recall, my own mother used to write names and dates on the back of our photos when we were kids. She always said it was to help her remember as we grew to be adults. "Kage, can I take a look at that? I want to see if there's anything written on the back."

He flips the frame over and shakes his head. "There's nothing."

"No, I mean on the inside. On the back of the photograph itself."

He holds my gaze, and I see the worry in them. "OK, but don't wreck it."

I smile weakly. "I won't. I promise."

I slide the plastic tabs aside, carefully removing the backing. Lifting the backing, I set it aside. The back of the photograph comes into view.

"Look," I whisper, turning it so Kage can see.

He squints. "I can't read that. What does it say?"

"It says—Miranda (26) and little Kage (3); with Aunty Amelia (24)."

"Aunty Amelia?" he says, curiously. "What?"

My eyes are wide, and Kage's words blur together. I can't believe what I'm reading. "We could ask Xander if he knows anything about it?" I suggest. Although it seems odd that he wouldn't have mentioned this to me earlier.

"Yeah, I guess." He shrugs.

"He's lived next door for a long time. Other than Amelia, and she has so much going on right now—he would have. Right?"

"Yeah, no. You're right, Marlys." He pauses for a moment, like he's thinking. "Can you text him to come over?"

I nod and send a message as requested.

It's not long before there's a knock at the door. Kage's impatient pacing has practically burnt a hole in the carpet.

He rushes to greet Xander, then drags him into the lounge room, already chewing his ear off about the box under the stairs.

"Here." Kage holds the photo frame in front of Xander.

I join them, sitting on the coffee table opposite.

"It's my mum," Kage blurts. "And Amelia." He waits a moment, then clears his throat. When he speaks, his voice is lower than usual, like he's trying to be a man. "Did you know they were sisters?"

"Sisters?" Xander appears as surprised as the both of us. "What on earth makes you think that?"

Kage explains the notation on the back, and offers to show him, but he declines, claiming he believes him.

"So, you didn't know, then?" I ask in a low voice.

Xander glances up, catching my gaze. There's a softening in his eyes, like he doesn't want to say what he knows. But then again, maybe I'm overthinking it. Placing meaning where there isn't any.

"No," he says, handing the photo back to Kage. "I never knew". But I'm still not convinced.

Kage continues to show Xander items from the box, sharing his excitement.

Suddenly, Kage quiets. Maybe these keepsakes are forcing him to relive his grief?

I glance at the clock. "I'm going to start dinner. Would you care to join us, Xander?"

"Yeah, that would be really nice." His words are tinged with sadness, and I brush my previous hesitation aside. He misses his neighbour—his friend. That's all.

An hour later, the three of us sit down to eat lasagne. We could all use some comfort food. The side salad is there too, but it's more so I don't feel guilty for the indulgence, than any health benefit.

Kage digs in like he hasn't eaten in days, which is a nice reprieve from the way he usually plays with his food before leaving it half eaten and storming from the table. Xander and I eat at a more casual pace, though I keep catching him staring at me every time I look his way. It's as if he's seeing me differently tonight, his lingering gaze glistening with secret intent.

It stirs my insides, and I think back to our previous romantic interludes. Is he thinking about that too?

Kage places his cutlery on his empty plate. "Do you mind if I go upstairs?"

"Uh, yeah, sure," I fumble with the words. He's never asked permission before, and for the life of me, I have no idea what's brought about this change now. He darts up the stairs, leaving Xander and I alone.

When we're done eating, Xander collects our dishes and shifts to the kitchen.

"Leave it, I'll do it later," I say.

"No, you cooked. I'll do these, it won't take long. You go find a movie." He rubs the back of his neck, hesitating. "Unless you want me to go."

"No," I blurt, faster and louder than necessary. "I mean, what do you feel like watching?"

He shrugs. "Whatever you feel like."

I narrow my gaze. "You know that means a chick flick, right?"

He laughs and waves me from the kitchen.

By the time I find a movie—a newish romcom just released on Netflix, Xander joins me on the couch. He stretches an arm along the backrest, brushing against my shoulder. It's cliché, like something I've seen in a thousand romance movies, but it sends a little ping in my chest all the same.

"You ready?" I ask, grinning broadly at him.

"Hit me with it," he jokes. I hit start and the movie begins.

As it plays, his ever-present stare wanders over me. His arm shifts, fingers grazing the back of my neck, playing with loose strands of hair. His caress reignites the spark I felt, when he kissed me on the front lawn. I shift in my seat, getting more comfortable.

"You alright?" he asks.

I nod, then rest my head on his shoulder, and focus on the movie as best I can.

Xander wraps his arm around me tighter and skims a finger along my shoulder, running down the curve of my arm. It's soft and delicate, and makes my heart race like I've just drunk ten cans of Red Bull.

I tilt my head up at him as he stares back down. There's no doubt I'm falling. Under his charms, under his spell, under his protective embrace. His jaw clenches, then releases, lips parting slightly as his eyes move between my gaze and my lips, hovering for a long moment. He searches my eyes again, asking for permission, and I give it silently, almost begging him.

Xander doesn't hesitate. His hands wrap around my waist, pulling me flush against him as he presses his lips against mine. Slow and deliberate, then his grip tightens, deepening the kiss. My hands slide into his hair, grip tightening. He moans, low and needy, urging me closer still. His fingers tease the edge of my shirt, grazing against my abdomen.

I pull back, placing a finger to his lips, lacing the fingers of my other hand with his, and stand. My sultry gaze says everything that's needed as I gently tug his hand. He follows eagerly, leading up the stairs and down the hall, until we reach my bedroom door.

Turning to face him, Xander grabs hold of me, like he wants to ravage me whole. He kisses me in kind, sucking every ounce of breath from my lungs, and pushes me against the door.

I smile against his lips, reaching for the handle, pushing it open.

My heart beats frantically against my ribs, like it might just up and burst out at any given moment. This is the part I like most. I always have.

The anticipation. The wanting. And that devilish look in his eye.

The part where I'm everything he wants—Hunter wants.

When he last made me feel this way. So very long ago. He'd want me to move on, right? But he was a selfish, conceited man in the end. He'd rather see me waste away into nothingness, forever alone, then allow my happiness to go on.

Fuck Hunter. Fuck every damn man just like him.

Why should they win? Why should we let them treat us this way?

Fuck, no. Not anymore.

Xander pulls back, eyes darting between mine. But I wrap both arms around his neck, pulling him towards me as I crash my desperate lips onto his. Moving backwards, I drag him with me, toppling onto the bed.

Today I choose me; I choose to be happy.

28

TOO LATE TO LIE

MARLYS

Every inch of my body, every nerve within, tingle as my mind replays each sensuous moment lost to the night. I'm acutely aware of this new level between us. I have my suspicions, but he won't say it. Not yet. It's too soon.

The eight-hundred thread count sheets cover my nakedness, warmed from the sun beaming through the sheer curtains. But it's the way the sun reflects off his stubbled jawline, bouncing from the curves of his eyelashes to the natural curl of his hair, that truly captures my attention. Every emotion pulsing through my body, like a sonnet daring to be penned.

He stirs, groaning as every cell of his body beams along with the morning. Rolling onto his side, his muscles bulge, pulling me closer. The touch of our noses, wakes him, eyes half slit as they barely open. In one swift move, he rolls me over onto my back, growling with the ravenous sound that tells me he wants me—maybe even needs me. For a moment, my heart beats heavy in my chest, waiting for his next move. My arms wrap around his neck, but before my lips reach his, he pecks a kiss on my cheek. Then the other. And finally, one on my forehead. He bounces from the bed, darting to the bathroom.

Thirty minutes later, I rap on Kage's bedroom door. "Breakfast in thirty," and practically float down the stairs to the kitchen.

Once the bacon is sizzling away, I fetch the eggs and bread for toasting. Standing in front of the stove top, arms wrap around my waist. Xander buries his head in the crook of my neck with a kiss, making me giggle like a schoolgirl.

"You're supposed to eat the bacon, not me," I tease.

"Can't I have both?"

I turn around, swatting him with a tea towel, but I can't wipe the grin from my face. "Watch it." I laugh, then turn serious. "Kage will be down here soon."

Xander rolls his eyes. "As if he cares." He grabs a mug from where he's seen me reach a thousand times before. "Coffee?"

"Please," I reply.

I plate up, then shift to the table.

"Mornin' sleeping beauty," Xander says to Kage as he shuffles his way towards us. "Any plans for the weekend?"

"Nope," Kage replies, sliding into the chair. He ruffles his already messy hair, and picks up a crispy piece of bacon, taking a bite.

I shake my head. "Nothing in particular. You?"

"I've got a delivery coming later. Stuff for the gazebo," Xander replies.

"It's completely done, then?"

"It will be once I get the seating and a few flower boxes in place."

"Maybe I'll come over later and check it out," I say, adding a wink for good measure. It's kind of cheesy, but I'm too giddy to care. Besides, Xander doesn't seem to mind, countering my wink with his own.

"Be sure you do," he replies.

"Gross," Kage blurts out. "If you don't mind, I'd like to enjoy my breakfast without this," he swirls a finger around, "lovey-dovey shit."

I stare wide eyed at Xander, trying to hold in my laughter, but it bursts out all the same. The high I'm riding today, well, nothing can get me down. Not even my sixteen-year-old stepsons attitude. I put an arm around him and pull him in for a quick cuddle. Though Kage wriggles himself away, rolling his eyes.

"Geez, Marlys. What the hell's gotten into you? You take some molly or something?"

"Molly?" I ask. "Who's that?"

Kage's brows rise high on his forehead. "It's not a who, it's a what," he deadpans.

I frown, still uncertain of his meaning. "What sort of what?"

"Oh my God, Marlys. You can't be serious?" he says, running a hand over his face. "How naïve can you be?"

I shrug, letting his jab about my innocence wash off me.

Xander reaches across the table, grabbing my hand. "It's a drug that makes you love everything and everyone."

"Oh," I say, finally understanding. But all my brain can focus on is the way his mouth formed that word. It's not quite how I'd pictured it. Something more personal, intended for me, rather than an explanation of drug effects.

"And just FYI," Kage says, "Your bedroom is not soundproof."

That familiar heat creeps up my neck again, and I desperately search for a reason to hide. I can't think of anything worse right now than having my sexual affairs exposed by a teenager.

My phone rings, vibrating against the table. Glancing at the phone number, my good mood stifles a little. It's been a few days since I've heard from the police and my mind reels with all the possible reasons for their call now. I snatch it up, standing from my seat.

"Sorry, I've got to take this. It's the police." Xander flashes me a concerned look before I turn away, heading down the hallway.

"Hello?" I say in a low, serious tone. An eerie feeling, like I'm being watched, sends all the hair on my arms standing on end, and a tingling sensation runs up my spine. I shiver.

The phone crackles with static, and for a second, I think I hear Hunter's voice, whispering my name. Then the static clears.

"Mrs Brannigan, I thought I'd give you an update of where we're at with the investigation," a deep male voice says on the other end of the line.

"Have you figured it out then? Who murdered my husband?" I ask, holding my breath as my pulse races faster. Yet an equal amount of hope that they've realised their suspicions of me—and Kage, for that matter—are incorrect.

"Our preliminary investigations have concluded, but the case remains open."

"What does that mean?"

"It means we've gathered all the evidence we could find and interviewed every person of interest..." his voice trails off.

"And?" I urge him to continue.

"And," he sighs heavily. "I'm sorry to say, that none of our lines of investigation have been fruitful as yet."

"You're still looking for the killer, though, right?"

The other end is silent for a moment before he speaks again. "The case is still open, but unless new evidence comes to light, I'm afraid we have nothing more to go on."

"What?" I spit out. "What about Brielle Maddox? And Grayson Whitmore? They're hiding something. How hard did you look at them?"

"Mrs Brannigan, I know this news isn't what you were hoping for. We looked into both of them, and a few other business associates of Mr Brannigan, and while we did uncover some shady dealings, there's no real proof that either Ms Maddox or Mr Whitmore committed this crime. Rest assured, we've passed on our findings to the appropriate authorities who deal with white-collar crime. They'll have to answer for those actions, just not murder."

I can't believe what I'm hearing. Hunter was an asshole who destroyed so many people, but he was still murdered by someone more callous than him. Who knows? Not the police, that's for damn sure. They're giving up. So much for justice.

"What now then?" I ask.

"Mrs Brannigan," he starts, then clears his throat. "I thought you'd be happy to have your name cleared, at least."

This is news to me. He hadn't actually said those words.

"Really? And what about Kage? He told me how he was bombarded with questions."

"Hmm, yes, well, you've both been cleared. The items seized from your home—"

"The Ratsak, you mean?" I interject, sharply.

"Yes," he says. "There was only one set of fingerprints on the box. Neither you nor Kage matched."

"And his body? Can you release him so we can finally have his funeral?"

"Yes, the paperwork is being signed off today, and we'll transport him to whichever funeral home you choose."

"Ok," I whisper, more to myself than the detective on the other end of the phone.

Our lives are moving on—mine, Kage, even Xander. Yet, Hunter's end remains the same, and without explanation. Some monster took his life and set me free in the process. It's only a matter of time until something surfaces. Or at least that's what I need to keep telling myself to make moving on alright.

The phone call ends without another word, and I head back to the kitchen. Chatter between Xander and Kage cuts off as I approach.

"Was that an update?" Xander asks. He crosses his arms and leans back in the chair. Kage watches me, waiting for an answer.

"Yes, and, no," I say. "The case is closed. Well, it's open, but they've run out of leads... apparently." I flop onto a chair at the table, defeated. "We've both been cleared though," I say to Kage. "That's something, at least."

"They're just giving up then?" Kage asks.

"Seems that way. At least we can start arranging your dad's funeral."

Kage stiffens and jaw clenches. I'm not sure if he's ever been to one, or whether this will be his first. Either way, it's going to be heartbreaking. I have to do everything I can to support him now. To get through this final stage. Then, maybe we can move on from this tragedy.

"I might go for a swim," Kage says, out of the blue.

I can't even remember the last time I took a dip. It's about time someone got some use out of it, other than the pool cleaner who comes every other week.

I nod. "I'll probably head to Xanders soon and help with the delivery, if you need me. Okay?"

"Sure."

A HOUR LATER I MEET XANDER BY THE GAZEBO AND take in the mass of items. There's much more than I'd originally thought and it's clear he's put a lot of thought into the project. Trays of seeds, cushions, and stacks of boxes. I would've bought a cast iron table with two chairs, and a few cushions, but it's like he bought half the store.

"Did you leave anything in the shop?" I say in jest, nudging Xander's elbow.

"Oh, she's got jokes, folks," he laughs.

"But seriously, where do we even start?" I ask, hands on my hips.

He rubs the stubble he didn't bother shaving this morning, with a finger and thumb. "How about I do the heavy lifting and put the seating together, and you can start getting those cushions opened. There should be some fairy lights around here... somewhere."

My brows pull together. "You don't think I can handle the putting stuff together bit?"

Xander grins and shakes his head. "I just thought your strengths were more in line with decorating than hard labour. Unless, of course, you've been hiding skills from me. How good are you with a drill?"

"Fine, fine. I get the point. Go do your thing, and I'll get the pretty stuff sorted," I say, waving him away.

But before he gets started, he wraps his arms around my waist, pulling me in close. He plants a subtle kiss to my lips, zapping any frustration that might've been sizzling under the surface, and tips his head so our foreheads meet. His eyes darken as I lose myself in them.

Xander's voice is low, sultry, as if he might swoop me up and carry me away. My mind unravels a little. Back to last night. "You're much too beautiful for sweat and dirt, Marlys." He pecks another kiss on my forehead, then lets me go.

For a minute, I watch him—his shoulders straining slightly as he hauls the heavy boxes towards the sullen structure. Right now, it's devoid of warmth, but with all this, I know it'll come together in the end. Xander gets to work, and so do I.

By the time he's finished assembling the outdoor furniture, I've arranged the cushions and throw and started winding fairy lights around the rafters. My shirt clings to my back, thick with sweat. Xander doesn't stop. He's nailed together all the planter boxes, positioned them along the perimeter, and filled them with soil. Earth and sweat cover every inch of his skin, like he's been rolling in it—yet my eyes drift to his abdomen, which is disturbingly attractive for a man in his forties.

He glances over, catching me in the act.

I fumble for an excuse. "Time for a break?"

He nods, while running his hands over the topsoil, smoothing it out. "I'll probably be another ten," he says, before wiping his brow with his forearm.

"I'll make coffee. Be right back," I say, turning towards the house.

I step through the mess of empty boxes and tangled plastic wrap on the patio, slide open the glass door, and head inside.

There's something strange about being in someone else's house alone. Like I'm overstepping or impeding on their secrets somehow. I'm probably just overthinking things again.

I brush it off and open two overhead cupboards before finding the coffee mugs. Grabbing a matching pair, I set them beside the kettle and click it on.

My stomach rumbles. Despite the big breakfast I made this morning; it must be getting close to lunchtime. The wall clock in the kitchen reads almost 1 p.m.—later than I'd realised. No wonder I'm starving.

Hopefully Xander has something snackable to go with the coffee. Cookies, perhaps.

The kettle rumbles in the background as I explore the walk in pantry for anything that resembles a biscuit. The top shelf is mostly dry goods–three types of pasta, two of rice, and a box of green tea that looks like it's been there since 2012. I move to the next shelf. A half-eaten box of stale crackers, an unopened box of protein bars, and a bag of mixed nuts closed with a plastic peg-type thing.

"Geez, Xander," I mumble under my breath. There's not a lot here as far as snacks go. I keep searching.

The next shelf has a large box of quick-cook oats in honey flavour, and two plastic jars of self-raising and plain flour. I giggle, as if he's ever baked a cake in his life. Beside that—a bag of sugar, a container of salt, and an assortment of food colourings and spices.

The next shelf is filled with cans, so I move to the very bottom shelf.

At the far end, hidden in the corner shadows, sits an old biscuit tin. The kind you get at Christmas with the blue enamel, and pictures of shortbread covered in sugar crystals on the front. My mouth waters. I haven't had one of these in forever.

It's weird that he's hidden it back here, but maybe it was

hidden to avoid temptation during a health kick. I pull it out.

Tugging at the lid, it comes off with a pop.

No cookies.

But something's inside.

I glance over my shoulder, confirming I'm still alone, before turning back to the tin.

Inside are two old jam jars. I reach in, pulling it out by its rust-tinged metallic lid. It's half full of blueish coloured pellets of some sort. I set it carefully on the shelf at eye level and grab the other.

The second one has a transparent liquid, tinted the same colour as the pellets. I swirl it gently. Small pieces of sediment lift and whirl like ash in water.

My stomach knots, and I lower the tin. Something inside shifts, clinking against the metal. I tilt the tin a little, and it comes into view, now resting askew inside the tin.

A knife.

My hands tremble, pulling it out slowly by its thin black handle. Dark reddish-brown stains mark the steel blade. My breath catches in my throat.

No. It can't be. I shake my head furiously trying to make sense of this discovery. This secret.

Xander's secret.

Footsteps sound behind me and I spin around. Xander is in the kitchen, just outside the pantry door, one hand on the doorframe. His gaze shifts from me to the biscuit tin on the shelf, then drops to the knife in my trembling hand.

He stills. My heart pounds heavy in my chest, pulse racing, telling me to get out of here. But I can't. He's standing in the one and only exit from the tiny space. This dungeon of hidden things.

"Marlys," he says, keeping his voice low and calm. His

arms are outstretched like he's trying to tame a wild animal. I step back, uncertain of everything. What to do. Who to trust. Where to go from here? My mind rattles with questions. The ones I really don't want to know the answer to. But here we are, evidence exposed. There's really only one thing to do now.

Tears well in my eyes, knowing the growing emotions I felt for Xander, will never be the same again. The trust I had. Gone. Vanished, never to be seen again. I hold his gaze, staring deep into his eyes, searching for even an ounce of truth. Of regret. Of something, anything, to make this less awful than it is right now.

His eyes—is it sadness or something else trying to fool me. But I can't let him bullshit me. Not now.

My voice trembles as I push the words out, terrified of what he might do. To me, with this knife. "Tell me this isn't what I think it is, Xander?"

His gaze shifts to the floor for a moment, then returns to me. "Just put it down, Okay? I can explain." He steps forward, I flinch, turning my head as if he might reach out and strike me.

His eyes change—like I've hurt him. Unbelievable.

"You think I would hurt you?" he says, quiet, barely above a whisper. "After... everything?"

Everything I want to say remains unspoken as my throat closes up, strangled by the weight of this unbearable truth. The knife was here. Hidden in his house. He did it. Or he's covering for who did.

"Marlys—"

"Just stop." My voice cracks. "Just stop talking." I edge sideways in the tight space, searching for an escape. My ears buzz, or like nails dragging down a chalkboard. I eye the doorway, and the small space to one side. Maybe if I run for it, I could squeeze through. I could get past him, then barrel for my house. Yes, that could work. I just have to wait for the right moment.

"Marlys, please. You know me," he begs.

"Do I?" I say, narrowing my gaze at him.

His jaw clenches tight. "I wanted to tell you. I tried, so many times. Just... give me a chance to explain. It's not what you think."

"It's not what I think?" I spit the words out. "I think you murdered Hunter and hid the evidence." My voice cracks, and my breathing is erratic. "You really had me fooled, Xander. I guess you fooled the police too, huh?"

Before he can respond, Kage's voice cuts through the tension.

"Marlys?" Kage calls out again, closer this time.

"Go home, Kage. Leave. Now," I scream, throat straining from the force. But it's too late. He appears behind Xander, in the kitchen. My eyes widen, darting between them, panic rising for Kage's safety. I can't let anything happen to him. Not now. Not ever.

"Kage, run. Call the police," I yell. "*Go now.*"

Xander turns halfway, blocking the doorway with his body. Kage shifts over to him. He's not running. He's not scared. They whisper—too low to catch—but they're calm.

What am I witnessing?

I don't understand.

Kage isn't frightened—doesn't look surprised.

No, he can't be in on this too. The possibility of the two of them, wrapped up in this murder together—it's too much. My mind screams to run. To make a break for it while Xander's back is turned.

I lunge, throwing all of my body weight forward, to barge through the doorway. My shoulder slams into his arm, and he stumbles, before acting on instinct. I make it only two steps into the kitchen, when he grabs hold of my wrist.

I scream, thrashing wildly. "Let go." But his grip only tightens, twisting my skin so it burns.

"Marlys. Stop."

I wrench hard with everything I have, feet slipping and skidding on the tile. I fall sideways into the frame, my head forcefully hitting something as I go down. My vision goes white for a moment as a sharp and unyielding pain spreads. The world tilts, and my heavy eyelids close, unable to fight any longer.

But just as the world is fading from view, I swear I see her.

Miranda.

Hovering over me like my guardian angel.

29

────────

EVEN IN RUIN

MARLYS

There's a dozen beating drums in my head, thumping a steady beat against my skull. I try to open my eyes, lashes fluttering, but the strain is too much, they settle shut again thrust into pitch-black darkness.

Under the covers, each muscle aches—from my neck, trailing down my spine, to my legs. I twist a little, trying to get comfortable, but a sharp pain in my lower back halts me.

It's unnerving. I've never had back pain like this before. And my head.

Pieces of my memory resurface. The tin. The jars. That bloody knife. And Xander. Oh my God, Xander.

A heaviness settles in my chest. What did he do?

And Kage. He was there too.

I try again, opening my eyes a little. A sliver of light runs across the familiar ceiling, and my gaze follows it to the window.

I'm home, in my bedroom. But I don't remember walking home from next door. I drag my hands up to my face, rubbing the sleep away. Beside me, I feel the bed depress as if someone has sat down. My hands fall, keeping my eyes shut, not wanting to know anymore. Maybe if I pretend this never happened, it'll all just go away.

A finger traces along my face, from my brow down to my jaw. They swish away my messy hair, uncovering my face. I try to act like I'm asleep, but I feel my brows pull together at the touch.

"Marlys? Are you awake?" The voice is barely above a murmur, so quiet, I might've thought it was in my head, except I know it too well. It's the same one that only a day ago, sent butterflies whirling in my stomach whenever he said my name. But now, it belongs to someone else. Someone I don't know, and never truly did. A liar. A monster. Wolf in sheep's clothing who fooled me. Xander.

My body stiffens, uncertain of my next move. After a long minute, he gets up from the bed, and I hear him set something down on the nightstand. Then a door clicks open and shut again.

Finally, I dare to take in my surrounds, and find a glass of water with some painkillers beside the bed. This small act of kindness could be a trick. These pills—maybe they're poison too. But my head hurts even more when I sit up. I swallow them followed by the water and lay back down for a few minutes so they take effect.

They do little to relieve the pain, now more of a thudding ache than a sharp jab, but I need to use the bathroom. Quietly I move to the ensuite, doing what I need to before washing my hands. I splash water over my face and look in the mirror.

I look like me. Same clothes, same eyes, same hair, only messier. But the longer I look, it's as if my reflection is slowly changing into something, or someone else. I examine the reflection further, turning my head one way, then the other. There's something I didn't see before. The similarities between me and Miranda. It's both uncanny and unnerving, resembling the one who came before.

Is this what Hunter saw when he looked at me? A second chance with his first love?

Maybe he saw it as an opportunity to right his past wrongs.

I place one hand on each side of the sink and hang my head. There's been so much change these past few months with Hunter missing, then found dead, finding out about Brielle, being treated like a suspect, then falling for Xander, and now what? I'm losing him too, and maybe even Kage. Everything I hold dear ripped away from me.

Tears well. I don't stop them. I've been trying to hold it together, to be strong, but I'm exhausted. Each drop of misery falls into the sink, swallowed by despair. With one hand, I wipe each cheek, spreading the tears over my skin so they glisten under the bathroom light. I return my gaze to the mirror, shaking my head as I wallow in self-pity. It's pathetic, but there's no hope anymore. I might as well just give up.

A recognisable cool shift fills the space and behind me something like smoke or mist whirls slowly, hovering. My eyes narrow on the mirror, watching the curls of transparent white form into a shape. A face. Mine? No, it's Miranda.

My lips form her name in a silent plea. Another billow of white shifts and rests on my shoulder, like a hand comforting a mourner. It's chilling, and my hair stands on end, but there's something else too. Different from the experiences I've had before. More like a calming presence, supportive even.

A voice so soft, almost like leaves rustling in a gentle

breeze, speaks. "Even in ruin, we bloom again. You will see."

The bedroom door clicks open, and the wispy white shadow fades into the air, gone. In it's place, Xander stands.

"Good, you're up. I was so worried."

I turn, dodging him as I scurry for the door, but Kage enters, closing it behind him, standing guard. I freeze in place, standing between the two of them.

Shit.

Xander waves an arm towards the bed. "Rest, please."

I frown, but I don't want any repeats of earlier, so I lay down, closing my eyes. The bed dips again, and I roll over, away from him. I'm his prisoner, but I'll be damned if I make it easy for him..

He rubs my back. "When you're feeling better, we should talk."

Talk? What a joke. Surely, he's not serious. What can he possibly tell me that I don't already know? A play-by-play perhaps, of how he planned the crime?

Kage shifts to the end of the bed. "You're safe now, Marlys. We both are."

I look at him but I don't recognise these words at all. I'm safe? I think not. He's been brainwashed into this story, that I have no interest in hearing. I close my eyes again, feigning sleep, hoping both will leave me alone long enough to figure out a way out of here.

Sleep isn't easy. Not with my mind racing, though eventually with the silence I'm swallowed into the darkness my body needs to recover. My dreams blur, except for one part. A repeat from the mirror. And Miranda, and those words.

Even in ruin, we bloom again.

She's right. Everything I thought I knew, now shattered

around me like razor sharp shards of fragmented glass. I could dwell on it, but that would just send me spiralling into depression, despair. Tormented for the sole reason I was too lazy to fight. Perhaps, her words are like a proverb. Maybe she's seen the future somehow. That things will work out, if only I push a little harder. Endure amongst the ruins of my life.

When I wake again, my head is better, only a dull ache remains, but my spirit has renewed. I'm ready. But for what, only time will tell.

The soft click of the door opening jolts my attention. It's Xander, again. This time his gift is coffee, and my body yearns at the smell of it.

"I wasn't sure if you'd be up," he says, sheepishly. Dark circles around his eyes and the way his shoulders slump, speak of exhaustion. He passes me the mug.

I hesitate, unsure whether this is another trick. He nods towards the cup, and I take it.

He sighs. "It's just coffee. I didn't drug you."

I frown, ignoring his response. "What time is it?"

"Early. It's just after six."

"In the morning?" I ask, and he nods. I slept so long—but obviously I needed it.

Xander drags a chair over and sits beside me as if I were a patient in the hospital. He sips his coffee, then lowers the mug to his lap, crossing his ankle over his other knee. "We need to talk," he says. His eyes search mine, but I look past him, refusing to give him the pleasure. "I need to tell you the truth, Marlys. All of it."

My gaze shifts back to him, narrowing cautiously, crossing my arms. "Really?"

"Yes. You deserve to know."

My arms remain firm, and my brows raise, disbelieving. "Okay then."

Xander's eyes shift to the floor and he clears his throat, thumbs fumbling with the mug in his hands. "I killed him," he says in a low voice, then raises one hand rubbing at his eyes, before lowering it again. Then he looks at me, more solemn and intent than I've ever seen before. "But I did it for you and for Kage."

I shake my head, slow and deliberate. I refuse to be the excuse for his crime. Opening my mouth to speak, he cuts me off, holding one hand up.

"Before you say anything, just hear me out. Okay?"

I roll my eyes defiantly the same way I've seen Kage do a hundred times before, and lean back against the bed rest. "Fine."

"He was doing it again. All the signs were there. The way he acted before... Miranda, and before Amelia." He shakes his head, rubbing the back of his neck. "He would have hurt you too, Marlys." His voice becomes more stern. "I couldn't just sit back and watch him destroy another innocent woman's life."

"You planned it, though," I deadpan.

"I did. It's not like I have experience with this sort of thing." He frowns. "At first, I couldn't sleep. Every night I was up trying to figure out how to convince you to leave him. Before it was too late. But no matter how much I tried, you kept using Kage as an excuse." He sighs. "And you were right, too. After Kage came to me, I knew he wouldn't be safe there alone with Hunter. He's just a kid, Marlys. How can he protect himself?"

I sit up straighter on the bed, leaning in. He had tried to tell me. How many times had he told me I deserved better?

And I had used Kage as my excuse, but it was valid. He sees that now, at least.

"I understand, but that doesn't make it right," I say curtly.

"I know," he says, then hesitates. "But... well," he sighs. "You have no idea of what he's put me through, too."

"No, you don't get to do that," I say. "You were going to tell me the truth, not come up with a bunch of excuses." Even I hear the harshness in my words, and for a small moment a pang of guilt hits, seeing the hurt in his eyes.

Xander shifts in his seat. "Sorry."

"Well?" I say, urging him on.

"You want to know how?" he asks, wincing. I nod but say nothing so he'll get to the point. "One night, I was watching TV when a field mouse ran through the lounge room. I knew you guys had problems with them a while ago, so I asked Hunter how he solved the problem. He gave me some of the RatSak, in a jar, to use at my place. It was more than I needed, so I just kept it there in case I needed it again."

"That doesn't explain how it got into Hunter's system though," I say.

"I was getting to that. I thought I could spike his drink or something, but those pellets, you can't hide that."

"The second jar," I say under my breath, realising now what it is.

He nods. "I diluted it into a liquid, so it was easier to... well, to get him to ingest it."

"So, you put that into his drink?" I can't believe what I'm hearing right now. It's as though I'm watching a crime show on TV, not hearing my husband's murderer recount his plot.

"Yes, that night after the dinner party. We had a few

whiskeys and beers while I was going over his business investment. At first, I didn't think it was affecting him. He just kept drinking, more and more, but then, he started feeling sick and ended up vomiting on my rug. It was a real mess." He shakes his head like he's remembering every minute of that night. After a long pause, he takes in a deep breath and continues. "After that, he just kind of passed out... on the floor, in the bathroom. He must've hit his head on the vanity going down. When I found him, he was slurring his words, but I could make out enough." Xander runs a hand down his face. "He was talking shit about you, Marlys. And me. Claimed he knew we were having an affair. Brielle... I heard her name too, but I couldn't make out what he was saying then. But I know what I heard. I tried to talk sense into him, to explain you and I, that we're just friends, but he wouldn't have a bar of it." His eyes shift to mine, holding my gaze, but it feels different somehow. More vulnerable. "He said he knew I was in love with you, that he saw it every time I was near you. And..." His gaze falls to the floor again. "He was right. But still, I didn't think you felt the same—we'd never been intimate, ever. I told him that. That he was wrong, but then he started calling you names. Awful things. Things that just aren't true. I got angrier, and angrier. I left the bathroom, tried to calm myself down. But while I was in the kitchen, all those things he said, well, they just kept repeating in my head." His jaw clenches, and closes his eyes briefly, before reopening them again. "There was a knife on the bench from where I'd cut a lemon for the beer. I wasn't thinking, I just grabbed it, and stormed back to the bathroom. He'd passed out again... or maybe he was dead, I can't be sure. But I plunged that knife into him—his chest, then lower. I would've kept going but..." He hangs his head, rubbing the back of his neck. "I thought

I heard her voice, telling me to stop. That he was gone, and Kage was safe."

"Wait," I say, focussed on him. "Who told you to stop?"

"I don't know. But I thought it sounded like Miranda," he says.

"But you said..."

He cuts me off. "I know. I can't explain it. All I know is that whatever it was, sounded an awful lot like her." He pauses and rubs at his eyes again. "Did you know we were friends?"

I shake my head. "Did you love her too?"

He lets out a little laugh. "I loved her like a friend, or maybe more, like a sister." Then his eyes grow darker, and voice lowers. "Not like the way I love you, Marlys."

I can't hear those words from him right now. All it does is confuse me. Maybe that's his intention. To manipulate me, so I won't dob him into the police. "Is that it then?" I snap.

"I wish that was it, but there's more. So much more." Xander gets up from the chair, and starts pacing around the room. He rubs his chin with his thumb and forefinger, like he's preparing for a speech. I watch him for a minute or two, before the tension becomes too much.

"Just tell me. It can't be worse than what you've already said."

He returns to his seat, leaning his elbows on his knees, and resting his chin on clasped hands. "The night Miranda died, he called me. It was late, after midnight. Hunter was panicking. Just kept saying he didn't mean it, and that he didn't know what to do. I couldn't even get a straight answer out of him. So, I came over. But when he let me in..." He shakes his head like he's remembering the details. "She was on the floor in the lounge room. I don't know how long she'd been like that, but her skin was already turning grey, except for her neck. He didn't tell me, but it was obvious he'd strangled her." Xander's eyes well with unshed tears, and it's clear how hard it must be, reliving this moment. "I wanted to call the ambulance and the police, but he convinced me that it was an accident. And that Kage needed at least one parent in his life. If Hunter went to prison, he'd be left as an orphan without anyone to love him. I couldn't do that to a three-year-old, Marlys. He was already going to struggle in life without a mother. I couldn't leave him without a father, too. But then he asked me to help him with her remains. He said he couldn't bury her at his house, in case the cops came looking for her. So, he asked if she could be buried in my yard."

I gasp. "Oh my God, you're not serious?"

"You don't understand. Back then, we were close—best friends even—but this was a whole different level of loyalty he was testing me with. I didn't want to do it, but I didn't know what else to do either."

"No, no, no," I whisper. "She's not... is she?"

He nods. "She is. Underneath the gazebo."

His tears fall. Not the kind you force out, but the kind that just happens, like his body can't hold it in anymore. Hunter had used him, manipulated him. Just like he had done with everyone. My stomach knots. How could he ask someone to do that? And why hadn't Xander told me this before? I would've understood–probably.

I consider everything Xander just told me. It's so very much to take in. He's a murderer, there's no question about that. But apparently, so was Hunter. My heart is heavy for the life Miranda lost, too. I can only imagine what that would have felt like. To have the life drained from you at the hands of one you love. I knew he had a temper, but what could she have done that would warrant such fury? Nothing. There's no excusing what he did. My mind drifts to Amelia, and how she'd ended up in the care home.

"And Amelia?" I ask. "What happened to her?" I narrow my eyes, to let him know I mean business. "You knew they were sisters, didn't you?"

Xander runs a hand down his face. "Yes, I knew. Not at first though. I thought she and Miranda were just friends. Every now and then, I'd see her when she visited. It was only after Miranda... well, you know... that I realised."

"I knew you were lying about that," I say.

"Yeah, sorry. I just didn't know how to explain everything else along with it."

"Tell me about Amelia, then."

He lifts his head and smiles as his mind wanders. "Amelia was so bubbly, always bouncing around, full of energy. The opposite of her sister, really. Miranda was more laid back, like nothing was ever too much trouble for her. But together, they balanced the other out." He smiles wistfully at the memory. "Anyway, Hunter made up this story that Miranda had left him—and Kage—she wanted a fresh start, or something like that. I never really paid too much attention to the excuse, because I knew the truth, as horrific as it was. But Amelia bought it, hook, line, and sinker. She loved her nephew, and Hunter was struggling since he'd never been much of a hands-on father. So, Amelia started helping out, kind of like a nanny, I suppose. But then Hunter did his thing, and before long she was under his spell too." He shakes his head. "I should have told her," he whispers.

The knowledge seems to weigh heavily on his shoulders. He's accepting blame that isn't his to bear.

Hunter should have been held accountable—for both Miranda, and whatever he did to Amelia.

"What happened?" I ask in a low voice, nudging him on.

His brows raise high, and he takes a breath, straightening his posture before relaxing again. "Almost the same thing. But this time, he'd hit her over the head with something, that's what caused her traumatic brain injury. Hunter thought she was dead, too, but luckily for her, she was still alive. Barely. When I told him..." He shakes his head. "He considered... finishing her off." He winces painfully. "But I managed to convince him otherwise. I got her the medical care she needed and made him believe it was better to hide her away than to kill her. In his eyes, there was no other option. He had the money, so I found the nicest care home I could, where she could live a nice life."

"And her family?"

"He made up some bullshit story just like he did with Miranda. Only this time, they were sceptical."

"Did she ever tell you why?" I ask.

He nods. "She suspected the lie about Miranda and started looking for clues. The more she searched, the more convinced she was that Miranda was dead and was haunting her and the house. But she couldn't find any actual proof to take to the police, so she asked Hunter— accused him." Xander runs a hand through his hair. "He wouldn't stray from his lie. He just kept saying it was all in her head until he got angry. And, well, you know the rest."

I nod, thinking it over. It's one thing to do those atrocities to Miranda and Amelia, but another thing entirely, to simply lie. And for what? To cover his tracks. So that he could live the perfect life. While others bathe in their grief. I missed all of Hunter's red flags. Fell for the lie he advertised. Just like the two women before me. I'm a fool, but at least I'm not alone. Maybe this is the reason Miranda's still here. Watching over Kage, loving him from a distance, ensuring his safety.

"Is that everything?" I ask, softly.

"Yes," he says matter-of-factly.

But then I remember. "What about Brielle? And Grayson? I honestly thought she was the one…" My words trail off. He knows my meaning.

A soft knock on the door then Kage comes in. He looks between Xander and me, like he's cautious of another blow up.

"Kage," I whisper, my mind trying to gauge how much he knows. How much this has all impacted on him.

"It's Okay. Come in," Xander reassures him.

Kage moves to the end of the bed and sits. "Are you alright now, Marlys?"

"Yeah, I'm fine. No need to worry." A small smile forms at the corner of his mouth, relieved. I turn to Xander. "How much of what you just told me, does he know?"

"All of it. I didn't want to but he insisted."

My lips draw into a straight line. I'm not sure that was the best decision, but it's done now, it can't be undone. I tip my head towards Kage. "How do you feel knowing everything?"

Kage shrugs his shoulders. "I've had a few weeks to process it all." Then his eyes dart away, like he's in trouble.

"A few weeks?" I blurt.

He flinches, like I slapped him on the face. "I didn't know for sure, but I suspected."

I watch him fidget. There's more he's not telling me, I'm sure of it. "What kind of suspicions?" I press.

"Well," he starts, "After Dad went missing, Xander was

different." He glances over at Xander who nods in approval to continue. And for the first time, I realise just how close these two have become. I kick myself, realising just how much I've not noticed. "He was a bit quieter than usual. And I could tell something was eating him up inside. 'Cos it's the way I act when I'm stressed out, too. So, I asked him."

My brows furrow. I can't believe it. "And he just told you?" I gaze darts between them, neither reacts.

"Yeah," he says, "But he didn't want to."

"But you insisted," I say, parroting Xander's words. He nods.

"We talked about telling you. I wanted to, but Xander thought you were already stressed out about Dad, and the cops, and finding out about Brielle. We thought it was better to wait. Until you were ready to hear it."

My heart caves a little. I'd been spiralling in my own grief while they both carried the truth. And on top, they thought they were protecting me. But were they? I don't know.

I stare at Xander. "So, what now?" I ask. "You can't keep me locked up forever."

"Now, it's up to you," he says.

"Me?" I ask. Xander nods. "So, if I want to go to the police, tell them everything, you're just going to let me walk out of here?"

He nods again. "If that's what you want, then I'll accept the consequences. All I ask is that you leave Kage out of it and take care of him."

This feels like a trick. No one would willingly go to jail. Would they? I look at Xander again. Really look. The man who held me in my darkest moments. Who reassured and supported me when I felt lost and alone. Who kissed my forehead, who loves me. And who buried my husband.

He's unflinching. Doesn't plead with me to save him from his fate. He's patient and waiting to see which way I'll go. With my heart, or with my head. But what if it doesn't have to be one or the other? What if justice isn't just about punishment? That won't bring back Miranda, nor heal Amelia's injury. And it won't rebuild what's left of me, either.

Perhaps justice isn't about what's right, but rather what we can live with.

I suck in a deep breath, holding it for a long moment before exhaling. I look at Kage, eyes wet, like he already knows the answer. Then I glance at Xander. I loved him. But do I still? As much as my head says it's stupid, everything in me knows I do. And it's that love—maternal for Kage, and all-encompassing for Xander—that I know what I must do.

We will never forget. But I can forgive. We can get through this, despite the weight of it.

Because, even in ruin, we bloom again.

30

IF I DON'T...

MIRANDA

I was wrong.

About Marlys, about Hunter, and most of all, about Kage.

After all this time focussing on what happened to me. Seeking revenge, and truth, and watching over my son. I see it now.

It's in the small fragments of things that her love prevails. The way she offers him a hug, the one I can't provide, even when he pushes back. How she simply serves his meal before hers and asks him how school was that day. Or the way an honest smile glides up her cheeks, basking in his happiness. Simple, mundane, but living life. Finding joy where there otherwise isn't.

I could feel guilty about haunting her and this house. But what good would that do? It's time to follow her lead and move on.

The tether has loosened, the light is waiting. All I need to do is follow. Despite the relief, not knowing what awaits is daunting. At least here, I know my limits. But I can't stay forever. At first, I didn't know what it was. It was jarring, not realising what changed. Then the dreaded truth, and the awfulness that came with it.

I had to make sure Kage was safe. And now Hunter's gone... he is.

She will care for him. Love him. Nurture him into a man. I don't need to hope; I see it. He'll take it all in his stride, make good where there isn't any. And be everything Hunter couldn't. I won't get to see him grow up, or make a life, a career, or family. But my faith is in Marlys now. To do what I'm unable, and be where I can't.

Before I go, I want to see him one more time.

Shifting to the lounge room, I hover on the edge.

Kage sits crouched on a round ottoman on the TV side of the coffee table, while Xander sits opposite on the couch, and Marlys on one side, legs underneath her as she sits on her feet. A board game covers the table between them, laughter shared as they take turns rolling the dice.

Marlys' small metal dog lands on a square. She shrugs, frowning dramatically, like a clown. Though Kage throws his hands in the air, screaming with excitement. She begrudgingly hands over a pile of play money.

The scene fills my heart with a warm sensation. But above all, it's abundant with love.

My gaze shifts to Xander. His usual restraint is even more so today. I'm not sure what it is, or why. Perhaps I missed something.

Marlys rests a hand on his thigh and smiles. His brows pull together as he picks her hand up and moves it back to the coffee table. He stands and strides toward the kitchen.

I've seen that look before. Not from him. From Hunter.

My stomach knots and I narrow in on Marlys. To see if she picked up on this flag. To me, it's as red as the tomatoes in his garden. Big and bold, and unmistakable. Though I hadn't read Hunter as easily. Both my sister and Marlys had missed them, too. But I've learned to read them now.

She smiles, returning her attention to Kage. Though her eyes don't seem as bright as before.

Xander returns, three glasses of something clear and bubbly in hand. He passes first to Marlys, then Kage, then sips from his glass before sitting back on the couch. Back to the game. Back to laughter, and family.

Maybe I misunderstood.

But then again, maybe I didn't.

I think back over everything—from this existence to the life I lived before. It's like a circle, isn't it? Once established, it's set in place, perhaps even for a lifetime. Each element, replaceable, but the cycle continues.

I was replaced by Amelia, then Marlys. But Hunter remained the same—the abuser. And the violence, too.

What if the roles have shifted again? What if Xander isn't the safe place they both think he is?

The thought is harrowing.

I can't leave. Not yet. Not without certainty. Any parent would do the same. I've gone to great lengths to protect my son, even when it seemed out of reach. Even without a voice, or a physical form, and no power to hold on to. I found a way. And I always will.

Just because I took my last breath within the circle—and Amelia almost did—doesn't mean I have to sit idly by and watch Marlys take her turn. Whether she sees it or not, someone has to break it. To stand up and say, "Enough". Because, if I don't... who will?

ACKNOWLEDGMENTS

This book would not have been possible without the unwavering support of so many people.

Firstly, to my parents, Ian and Lynelle, who encouraged me to pursue my dream of becoming a writer; and to my sisters, Alison and Anne, who may not always understand everything I've been through but have always cheered me regardless.

To my beautiful children, Ethan, Isaac, Jordyn, and Gabriel—thank you for always having my back, for encouraging me to chase my dreams, and for listening to me talk about my books for hours on end, even when you couldn't bear to hear another word. Your constant support means everything.

To my dearest friend, Nancy—you have been my biggest supporter from the very beginning; you read every word, every painstaking chapter, and encouraged me to keep going without ever asking for anything in return. Your unwavering friendship and steadfast loyalty kept me sane when life put me through the wringer, despite your own loss and grief. Words cannot express how incredibly grateful I am for your friendship—thank you.

I also want to thank my editor, Joanna St. Amour, who has been patient and kind, and helped polish this book into something worthy of sharing with the world—and for shouting about my debut.

And I can't forget my skilled and multifaceted cover

designer, Tash from DAZED Designs, who was there at every turn—from creating this amazing cover design to the blurb and formatting—and for your friendship and guidance through the indie publishing process.

To all of you who gave this new writer a chance—whether you beta read, offered critique, or joined the ARC team—thank you for investing your time, thoughts, and energy into my debut. From the depths of my heart, thank you.

And lastly, a huge shout-out to every one of you who picked up my book and gave it a chance, and to those for whom the book's theme resonates—I wish you love, peace, and joy, wherever you are on your path. Always remember, in the depths of ruin, you will bloom.

ABOUT THE AUTHOR

I live in sunny North Queensland, Australia, with my furry pals, Ollie, and Angus (Shih Tzu's) and their mortal feline enemies. In my downtime, I enjoy spending quality time with my family, chill out watching Netflix, or read something new from my TBR list. My favourite reads are an eclectic mix of thrillers, romcoms, cosy mysteries, post-apocalyptic stories, and a little horror. My own stories revolve around haunted homes, secrets, betrayals, and the people we trust most - until we don't.

Visit My Website
www.kgjessupwriter.com

instagram.com/kgjessupwriter
facebook.com/kgjessupwriter
tiktok.com/@kgjessupwriter
threads.com/@kgjessupwriter

ALSO BY K. G. JESSUP

COMING SOON
'The Name You Gave Me'